BETH CORNELISON

started writing stories as a child when she penned a tale about the adventures of her cat, Ajax. Since that first time, Beth has written many more stories of adventure and romantic suspense and has won numerous honors for her work. She loves reading, traveling, Peanuts' Snoopy and spending downtime with her family. She writes from her home in Louisiana, where she lives with her husband, one son and two cats who think they are people. Beth loves to hear from her readers. You can write to her at P.O. Box 5418, Bossier City, LA 71171 or visit her Web site at www.bethcornelison.com.

SHARRON McCLELLAN

began writing short stories in high school but became sidetracked when she moved to Alaska to study archaeology. For years, she traveled across the United States as a field archaeologist specializing in burials and human physiology. Between archaeological contracts she decided to take up the pen again and soon discovered Romance Writers of America. In 2002, she sold her first novel. Sharron now blends her archaeological experience with her love of fiction. To learn more, visit her at www.sharronmcclellan.com. She loves to hear from her readers.

JENNIFER MOREY

has been creating stories since she fell in love with *The Black Stallion* by Walter Farley. She has a BS in geology from Colorado State University and is now program specialist for the spacecraft systems segment of a satellite imagery and information company. Jennie has received several awards for her writing, one of which led to the publication of her debut novel, *The Secret Soldier.* She lives in Loveland, Colorado, with her yellow Lab and golden retriever.

BETH CORNELISON
SHARRON McCLELLAN
JENNIFER MOREY

Blackout at Christmas

Silhouette®
Romantic
SUSPENSE

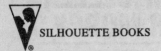

SILHOUETTE BOOKS

ISBN-13: 978-0-373-27653-0

BLACKOUT AT CHRISTMAS

Copyright © 2009 by Harlequin Books S.A.

The publisher acknowledges the copyright holders of the individual works as follows:

STRANDED WITH THE BRIDESMAID
Copyright © 2009 by Beth Cornelison

SANTA UNDER COVER
Copyright © 2009 by Sharron McClellan

KISS ME ON CHRISTMAS
Copyright © 2009 by Jennifer Morey

Visit Silhouette Books at www.eHarlequin.com

Printed in U.S.A.

CONTENTS

Dear Reader,

What better way to keep warm on these brisk November nights than with this month's adrenaline-pumping romances from Silhouette Romantic Suspense?

What would you do if the lights went out at Christmas? Three stellar authors—Beth Cornelison, Sharron McClellan and Jennifer Morey—contribute heartwarming stories to our *Blackout at Christmas* (#1583) anthology, which features three couples as they fall in love during a Seattle blackout. Also available this month, you won't want to miss the second book in the author-led miniseries TOP SECRET DELIVERIES, *The Cowboy's Secret Twins* (#1584), by Carla Cassidy. Here, a single mom unwittingly finds herself at the home of her babies' father, who then has to keep them out of harm's way.

Popular author Linda Turner begins her new family-themed miniseries THE O'REILLY BROTHERS with *His Wanted Woman* (#1585), which involves danger and romance in our nation's capital. You'll love Sheri WhiteFeather's sexy beginning to her miniseries WARRIOR SOCIETY, *Imminent Affair* (#1586), where a noble hero with amnesia protects the woman he loves from a deadly threat.

These romances will definitely keep you toasty this month. As always, we deliver on our promise of breathtaking romance set against a backdrop of suspense. Have a wonderful November and happy reading!

Sincerely,

Patience Smith
Senior Editor

STRANDED WITH
THE BRIDESMAID

Beth Cornelison

To Patience Smith, Jennie Morey and Sharron McClellan—
thanks for making this project such a
fun and rewarding experience. Merry Christmas, ladies!

Chapter 1

"*D*ue to inclement weather conditions, all flights for Seattle-Tacoma International Airport have been canceled until further notice. Please see your airline service agent for further assistance."

Ellen Davis suppressed a groan as the airport public address system repeated the grim news that had her, and eighty gazillion other holiday travelers, standing in line to rent a car two days before Christmas.

Next in line to speak to the car rental agent, she refused to give in to the frustration and aggravation gnawing at her. Everyone was tense and grumpy because of the inconvenient weather, but if it killed her, she'd maintain the pleasant holiday cheer that those around her seemed to have forgotten.

The tall man in front of her took the key to his rental and the folder of papers he was handed and stepped aside. Ellen moved to the counter while he glanced over and signed his rental agreement.

"I need whatever you have left. I'm not picky as long as it has wheels and can get me to Spokane by tonight," she told the frazzled woman behind the desk.

From the corner of her eye, she noticed the tall man glance up at her. While the rental agent tapped her computer keys, Ellen cast him a polite glance, caught his eye and smiled.

Dark-haired, lean and oh-so-handsome in his suede bomber jacket and faded jeans, he returned a lopsided grin and continued to watch her. Ellen's stomach did a jittery dance under his perusal.

"Looks like we have a Taurus or—"

Ellen turned her attention back to the rental agent when she spoke, conscious of the man's lingering gaze. "I'll take it."

"Or for just ten more dollars I can put you in a—"

Darkness swallowed the room.

With a flicker and a collective groan from the horde of weary travelers, the power blinked out. Halogen emergency lighting struggled on throughout the terminal, casting the reservation lobby in a surreal dim glow.

Ellen squelched the flutter of panic that tickled her gut. Soon she'd have a car, and with luck, she could still make her sister's wedding rehearsal dinner tonight if—

"I'm sorry, ma'am." The agent frowned and banged her keyboard. "I lost my computer when the power failed. I can't access our database."

"So just give me the Taurus you mentioned. That's fine." She tapped her toe nervously, anxious to simply get on the road before the freak snowstorm pounding Seattle got any worse.

"I can't do that. Without the computer, I can't rent anything else today."

"Excuse me? You just said you had a Taurus." Hearing the tension that had crept into her voice, Ellen gritted her teeth so hard her jaw ached. She battled down the rising stress and tried again. "Can't you do the paperwork by hand? You know you have the car, so—"

The woman was already shaking her head, her expression hard and unsympathetic.

The agent's apparent lack of concern for her predicament and the plight of the other stranded travelers frayed Ellen's last nerve.

"Then how am I supposed to get to Spokane? Do you have any idea how upset Trixie will be if I miss her wedding?" Her voice trembled, and tears of frustration and disappointment tightened Ellen's throat.

The car rental agent gave her a bored look. "That's not my problem."

Ellen saw red. Forget patience and holiday cheer and a spirit of cooperation during a crisis. She was ready to climb over the counter and throttle the rude woman.

"What?" she snapped. Her hands shook as she struggled for a calming breath.

Down the corridor, an alarm blared, and the grumble of the crowd behind her spoke for the growing unrest in the airport.

"Excuse me." A warm, steady hand gripped her elbow, and Ellen pivoted to face the handsome man…who'd gotten the last car before the airport lost power. "Did you say you were going to a wedding? In Spokane?"

Ellen knitted her brow. "I— Well, yeah. How'd you—"

"Trixie Davis and Sean O'Banion?"

She blinked, stunned. "Yes. Why?"

A broad dentist-perfect grin spread across his face. "I'll be damned. Me, too. Would you like to ride with me?"

A startled laugh hiccupped from her throat. "You're going to Trixie and Sean's wedding, too?"

He held out his hand. "Zach Kallen. Sean's best man."

Ellen gaped. "No way!"

"Way." He smiled again, a dimple pocking his cheek, and her pulse danced.

Exhaling the knot of oxygen that had been logjammed in her chest since the airport closure was announced, she nodded. "If it's not too much trouble, yes. Please. I don't think I'm going to get there any other way."

Zach gathered his backpack and slung it over a shoulder.

"Then follow me. I'd like to get over the mountains before they close the highway."

Ellen gathered her purse and wiggled through the press of bodies clogging the lobby in front of the rental desk. Aggravation and desperation were written on the faces of the people still waiting to find a way to reach their loved ones for the holidays. When she caught up to Zach, she gave him another appreciative smile. "Thank you. You're my hero."

He shrugged. "It only makes sense to share a ride if we're headed the same place."

"Just the same...you're a lifesaver." She jogged to keep pace with his long-legged strides and gave the dim corridor an uneasy glance. The watery gray light that seeped through the large windows along the terminal did little to dispel the pervading gloom the snowstorm and power outage cast.

They passed a large Christmas tree in the airport lobby as they headed outside. The darkened strands of lights and shifting shadows filled Ellen with a hollow ache. Twinkling lights brought life and beauty to a Christmas tree. Without the strings of lights ablaze, the tree seemed lonesome, dead and dreary. She prayed this holiday weekend, and especially Trixie's wedding, didn't fall victim to the snowstorm like the tree, losing their sparkle and joy. Already the blackout and bad weather threatened to ruin the occasion for Ellen.

"I don't know what I'd do if I missed my sister's wedding," she said breathlessly, trying to keep up with Zach. "We've been dreaming of this day since we were old enough to dress our Barbies in white dresses and practice writing Mrs. in front of our names."

Zach tossed a disgruntled look over his shoulder. "Been on the husband hunt awhile, have you?"

"I didn't say that. You make us sound desperate or calculating. But most girls dream of a fairy-tale wedding to the man they love long before they know who that special someone will be. And Trixie and I have put hours into planning her wedding. If I miss it—"

"You won't." He gave her an even look, full of assurance. "I'll get us there one way or another."

His confidence calmed a few of the jitters dancing along her nerves. As they stalked past the luggage carousels, she sent the conveyers a longing glance. "I guess snagging my luggage is out of the question, since I checked it through to Spokane."

"Which is why I always carry my bag with me." Zach patted the backpack on his shoulder and gave her a self-satisfied grin.

"A carry-on wouldn't have worked for me. I was packing for a week, including the wedding and all that entailed. My bag weighed a ton." Ellen dodged a frazzled-looking family and sent the mother a sympathetic smile. Getting stranded in a powerless airport this close to Christmas had to be a parenting nightmare.

Zach slowed his pace momentarily, allowing Ellen to catch up. "Never fear. Your suitcase will be sent on as soon as the airport reopens and flights resume."

She pulled a face, unconvinced. "I can hope. That won't help me for the next day or two, though."

When they stepped out of the terminal and headed into the parking garage in search of the rental car, a blast of wintry wind slammed into them. The chill sank all the way to her marrow.

Without the security lights, the lower levels of the parking garage were as dark and cold as a tomb. Only the occasional moan of the storm winds in the rafters broke the eerie stillness. As if, because of the blackout and the snowstorm, all of Seattle had fallen into a deathlike slumber. A chill raced through Ellen, wholly unrelated to the ice pellets peppering the streets or the arctic wind whipping through the rental level of the parking lot.

Picking up her pace, she inched closer to Zach's solid build. In his wake, the scent of leather and pine filled the air, and Ellen inhaled the heady aromas. In addition to his chiseled features and startlingly blue eyes, Zach walked with a confident, loose-limbed stride that exuded strength—and perhaps a tad of arrogance.

When a skittering sound rustled in the shadows, another uneasy jitter crawled up Ellen's spine. She determinedly focused on Zach's sexy walk and broad shoulders rather than the biting cold, the dark garage and the nip of foreboding the nasty weather stirred in her.

While she was lost in thoughts of her companion's snug jeans, her foot hit an unexpected patch of ice. She grabbed for the bumper of the nearest car to catch herself—triggering the shrieking wail of the car's security alarm. With a gasp, Ellen jerked away, her nerves jumping. Again her feet skidded on the slick ice. This time, Zach appeared at her side in a heartbeat, catching her under her arms and hauling her up against the solid wall of his chest.

Ellen sank her fingers into the warm suede of his coat and raised an embarrassed grin. "Oops," she shouted over the loud alarm.

He quirked an eyebrow but didn't release her. She made no move to pull away, either. The wide span of his hand at the small of her back, anchoring her close to his sturdy frame, suffused her with a sense of safety and comfort when so much else had gone wrong today.

What would she have done if Zach hadn't been standing in line with her, hadn't offered to share the rental car? She'd be stranded here in a city with no power while her sister walked down the aisle. Shoving the dreary thought aside, she squared her shoulders.

He arched one dark eyebrow and gave her a measuring glance that sent a tickling warmth to her belly. "You okay? Got your land legs back?"

"Yeah, thanks." Even though standing snuggled securely in Zach's arms had tremendous appeal, she stepped back.

His expression sobered. "A guy at the gate had a radio, and I heard him tell his friend the authorities were trying to keep I-90 through Snoqualmie Pass open as long as possible. But if the storm doesn't ease up, the interstate could be closed soon. Even if the roads are open, driving will be tricky."

Zach's warning revived the knot of anxiety that sat in her chest.

"Then I guess we need to hurry if we are going to reach Spokane in time to help Trix and Sean celebrate their marriage." When Zach's face grew dark, Ellen hesitated. "What is it, Zach?"

"You may be going to celebrate with your sister, but my rush has nothing to do with revelry. I'm going to Spokane to save Sean from making a big mistake. I'm going to stop the wedding."

Chapter 2

"Excuse me?" The stunned expression Ellen gave him was almost comical. Almost.

Except that Zach was dead serious about saving his best friend from an ill-advised commitment. He turned without answering her and continued down the unlit row of cars, squinting into the darkness to find his rental.

"Zach, wait!" The clatter of Ellen's high heels on the cement—what had she been thinking with that shoe choice in weather like this?—echoed off the garage walls as she hurried to follow him.

"I know you want to debate my reasons for going to the wedding," he said without breaking stride, "but can we do it in the car? The storm won't hold off while we argue over the wisdom of this wedding."

Spotting the white sedan in the correctly numbered parking spot, Zach pulled out the key fob and clicked off the door locks. He tossed his backpack on the rear seat, then opened the passenger side door for Ellen.

She stopped at the rear bumper and braced a hand on her hip. Even in the dark garage, he could tell her glare shot daggers. "Stop the wedding? Are you insane? You said you were Sean's best man!"

"And as such, it is my job to look out for his best interests. In my opinion, that means convincing him *not* to say, *I do*." He motioned for her to get in the car.

She didn't budge. "Trixie is what's best for Sean. They're in love!"

Zach sighed. "Can we debate that point on the road? Time's wasting."

Ellen marched closer and stuck her face in his. A sweet, floral scent swirled around him, teasing his nose. Her eyes flashed with green fire, and her ivory skin flushed with ire. "I won't let you do this to my sister. You're—"

Zach kissed her. Just a quick smack on the mouth, but it served his purpose. He derailed her argument, stopped her talking. He'd taken one look at the pout in her plump, raspberry lips and given in to the impulse.

Ellen blinked at him, a stunned, quizzical dent in her brow.

"Get in, please. We'll talk as we drive."

She drew an unsteady breath and released it slowly, her wary gaze taking stock of him. Finally she ducked her head and climbed in the front seat. As Zach rounded the front bumper, he cut a side glance through the windshield in time to see her press her fingers to her lips. As if her mouth still tingled from his kiss.

He squashed the urge to imitate her gesture, though the effect of that short, tactical kiss still sizzled through his system. The taste and feel of her lips rocked him to his core.

Steady, boy. You need your best game on to tackle these icy roads. Don't let a tempting bridesmaid distract you from the task at hand.

Zach pulled out of the parking garage and into the pinging snow and sleet that had brought all of Seattle to a halt and knocked out power. Until the storm cleared and the utility company could get the lights back on, Seattle was in for a messy, inconvenient Christmas holiday.

He gritted his teeth as the front tires of the Malibu he'd rented lost traction for a moment. Thanks to the storm tracking from Seattle across the Cascade Mountains, he faced a tedious, treacherous drive to Spokane.

"Do we have snow tires?" Ellen cast a dubious gaze at the dark clouds that spit icy precipitation. Her face reflected the same concerns churning through him.

"Doubt it. They're generally not needed in Seattle, so rental companies don't put out the bucks."

He took the steep driveway of the parking garage slowly and merged onto the main access road leading away from the airport. Traffic was almost nonexistent.

Anyone with a brain was hunkered down at home rather than tackling the icy roads.

He'd have loved to be one of the saner people perched in front of his TV with a whiskey-spiked eggnog and the Seahawks game. But Sean had been his best friend for too long for Zach to miss his wedding. To miss one last chance to talk some sense into his buddy.

What was Sean thinking, giving up the single life for monogamy, a mortgage and holidays at the in-laws? How could commitment to one woman possibly compare to the freedom of bachelorhood? Did Sean really think marriage led to happiness? Had his friend bought into the fairy-tale hype of happily ever after? Zach suppressed a groan. He'd seen too many marriages fail, too many unfaithful spouses, too much deception, corruption and cynicism to foster such an idealistic view.

"Okay, we're in the car. Care to explain what you meant about stopping my sister's wedding?" Ellen asked before they'd even reached Interstate 90 toward town. "What did Trixie ever do to you that you'd want to ruin her wedding? Which—" she aimed a finger at him "—I won't let you do, by the way."

Zach approached an intersection where the traffic lights were out. Other cars approached then haphazardly darted through the crossroad. After waiting his turn, Zach started across, only to jam on the brakes when another car zipped out in front of him. The lightweight sedan he'd rented fishtailed.

Ellen gasped and clutched her seat belt.

The other car honked, swerved around them and zoomed away.

Sighing, he squeezed the wheel in frustration. "When the light is out, you treat an intersection like an all-way stop, dude. Get with the program."

Ellen chuckled and sent him an amused grin. "I talk to other cars as I drive, too."

He shrugged. "Stupid habit, really. They can't hear you. Don't know why I bother."

"Because it makes you feel better? I bet you talk to the TV, too. Am I right?"

Zach checked his blind spot over his left shoulder as he merged onto the interstate, then cut a side glance to Ellen. "Only when I watch sports. And only when the refs get the call wrong. Or the players make a boneheaded mistake."

Amusement lit her face, and she settled back in her seat. "Yeah, right."

He flashed a quick grin, but when her unanswered question filtered through his mind, he sobered. "I have nothing against your sister. I'm sure she's very nice. But I know Sean, and I know he'd be happier if he stayed single."

Ellen scowled. "Apparently not. He's the one who proposed."

"Trixie was probably pressuring him, dropping hints, making ultimatums…."

"Wrong." She shifted on the seat to face him. "He's happy. I've seen them together, and this is what they both want. Don't interfere!"

"He may think it's what he wants, but in a few years, he'll get restless. He'll feel trapped. Or she will."

She scoffed her disagreement and shook her head.

"One of them will cheat," he continued, "and the other will find out. Or not…and then the cheater will be miserable, because they're carrying around a load of guilt. They'll drift apart, be unhappy, get divorced…or not. Maybe they'll continue a charade of a marriage for the sake of the kids or for appearances in society or some other bull reason." Zach clenched his teeth, shoving down the sour spike of resentment and disillusionment that churned in his gut. Heaving a weary sigh, he dug the antacids from his pocket and, with his thumb, he popped a couple from the top of the roll into his mouth.

Ellen said nothing for a moment, but the weight of her stare bore into him like icy stakes. Why had he vented like that? If anyone knew better than to rant in public, he did. His job was all about discretion, keeping a lid on all the ugliness that he encountered every day.

Finally, crossing her arms over her chest, Ellen tipped her head and furrowed her brow. "Jaded much?"

"I just call 'em as I see 'em."

She nodded sagely. "Ah, so this is the voice of experience speaking. You were married, and it went bad."

"Nope. Never been in a long-term relationship."

"Parents had a bitter divorce?"

He rolled his shoulders uneasily. She was getting too personal for comfort. But then, he'd brought the subject up. *Big dummy. Should've kept your yap shut.* Zach tightened his grip on the steering wheel—but not because of the road conditions. Considering the unexpected ferocity of the winter storm, the road crews had done an admirable job of clearing the lanes on the interstate in town. Snoqualmie Pass would be another matter.

"My folks divorced, but it wasn't especially bitter. None of my mom's four divorces were too acrimonious."

"Your mom divorced four times?"

Zach winced internally. He hated the sympathy he heard in Ellen's tone. He wasn't looking for pity for himself or his mother's misguided choices. Besides, his mom's numerous trips down the aisle weren't the root of his ill view of marriage. "Two of them from the same guy. You'd think she'd have learned the first time."

The heartbroken expression Ellen wore when he glanced at her twisted inside him. "What's that look for?"

"You must have had a tough time growing up, having your mom remarrying and divorcing so often."

"My childhood was fine, thank you. Look, can we change the subject? You're making a mountain out of a mole hill."

"It's not a mole hill if, because of your bleak opinion of matrimony, you intend to spoil my sister's big day and shatter her dreams."

"I'm not—"

The truck in front of them spun out on an icy patch, and Zach's reply dashed from his brain. Adrenaline ripped through him, jacking up his pulse, as he took evasive action. He cut the wheel left, avoiding the truck, then hard right again to miss hitting the median wall and the van in front of him. The Malibu's wheels slipped, and the rental car careened sideways toward the shoulder.

Chapter 3

They skidded several yards before Zach could regain control of the car.

Once they'd regained traction, Ellen exhaled the breath she'd held as they slid all over the highway. Thank God there wasn't much traffic or… She shuddered. She didn't think she would take another easy breath until they were safely at the church in Spokane. Or, considering Zach's determination to change Sean's mind, she wouldn't rest easy until they were toasting the newlyweds at the reception.

Ellen glanced at Zach's chiseled profile and the tick of the muscle in his jaw. "So…if not because of your parents, why do you have such a dim view of marriage?"

He cast her a withering glance. "Are we still on that? Can't we talk about something else?"

"No. I need to know why you're determined to come between two people who clearly love each other. All you have to do is see the way they look at each other, and it's obvious what's in their hearts."

He grunted. "That's a very...Hallmark-card sentiment. And for what it's worth, I never said I wanted to break them up. I just think marriage adds something that burdens the dynamic of the relationship."

Ellen gaped at Zach. "You mean something like commitment? Security? Faith and trust? Yeah, those are real *burdens!*"

His jaw tightened, and he flicked an irritated glance her way. "You can have all those things without complicating the relationship with legal contracts and a certificate from the state."

Ellen leaned her head back against the seat, appraising him, studying his taut jaw, the frown lines that pulled at the corners of his mouth. Her pulse kicked up. That mouth had shock her, tantalized her. His kiss had tasted like cinnamon and hinted at buried passion. So how could a man whose kiss could warm her from the inside out have such a cold attitude toward love and marriage?

And then it hit her. "You've never been in love, have you? Not truly, deeply, change-your-life in love?"

He snapped a startled glance her way, but said nothing for a long time. "No."

A prick of sadness pinched her heart, even as understanding released the knot of frustration inside her.

"That's what I thought." She turned her gaze out the side window, watching the darkened houses and sleet-crusted trees they passed. The stab of melancholy she felt for Zach dug deep, weighing down her heart. Sighing, she closed her eyes. "Until you've been there, until you've known what it is like to have another person be at the root of every breath, every thought, every fiber of who you are, there's no point in arguing the merits of marriage with you."

"Does that mean we can change the subject?"

She didn't bother answering. Except for the swish of the windshield wipers and pinging of the snow and sleet on the windows, they rode in silence for several minutes. Finally, they reached Interstate 90 and merged with the other traffic headed east out of Bellevue.

Ellen spotted a few lights still on, but figured it was only a matter of time before the entire city was in darkness. Just in time for a long, cold night. She shivered involuntarily, wishing she hadn't had to stay at work yesterday to finish laying out the special holiday edition of *Portland Today,* the regional magazine she'd written and edited for since college. She'd give anything to be in Spokane already with Trix and her parents, finishing the last-minute details of the wedding and enjoying a cup of her mother's hot cider.

Ellen was fully immersed in a daydream about Christmases past with her family when Zach broke the silence. "It's just that everywhere I look, I see married people who are unhappy for some reason." He turned up one palm on the steering wheel as he drove. "I see men cheating on their wives, being eaten alive by the guilt, then ruining their lives and professional reputations tiptoeing through minefields of deception. I deal daily with women who can do nothing but complain about their husbands' faults and their kids' bad attitudes. Meanwhile, it's my job to put a good face on all the yahoos, run interference and save careers that would be in the toilet if the public knew what really happened behind closed doors." He huffed a sigh of disgust and cast Ellen a frustrated sideways glance. "So, yeah, I'm jaded. I see the worst of people more than anyone should, because it's my job to fix my bosses' messes."

She tugged up a corner of her mouth. "I thought we were changing the subject."

Color rose in his cheeks, making his already handsome face even more appealing. His tirade and his telltale flush echoed her suspicion that Zach suppressed a lot of passion beneath his cool facade.

"You asked where my opinion of marriage came from, so…now you know."

"The people you work with."

He squeezed the steering wheel again, his knuckles blanching. "Yeah."

"And what is it you do? Where are you working with so many unhappy people?"

"Sacramento. I'm on the PR staff for a California state senator. Whoever said politics made strange bedfellows must have been on a senator's staff and seen what I've seen. It's enough to knock the idealistic grin from any political science major's face."

Ellen tipped her head, flabbergasted. Rather than bitterness, his tone rang with a hopeless, world-weary dejection. "Good grief, Zach. If you hate your job so much, why do you stay on?"

"Because." He lowered his eyebrows and pressed his lips in a stubborn scowl. "Quitting means admitting defeat. I got into politics because I wanted to make a difference. I thought I could do something good, something worthwhile. I haven't given up on the hope that maybe I can do something important for my state and make a change for the better."

She grinned again and squeezed his shoulder. "So this particular political science major hasn't completely lost his idealism?"

He blinked his surprise then held her gaze for a moment. "I…guess not. It's just so damn frustrating to know perfectly good legislation gets ruined by backroom deals and partisan fighting and…personal agendas."

"And those personal agendas would include the reasons you are so down on marriage?"

Zach dragged a hand through his hair, leaving it rumpled and sexy. Blowing a deep breath through pursed lips, he narrowed a troubled gaze on the icy road. "I shouldn't have said anything. Please don't repeat any of this. I had an especially bad day yesterday and—"

"Okay. This will all stay strictly off the record, if…"

He arched an eyebrow when she hesitated. "If what?"

"Promise me two things."

He gave her a wary look. "What?"

"Promise me you'll at least consider finding a new job. There are other ways to make a difference and change public policy without losing yourself and your ideals to the political machine."

The muscle in his jaw jumped. "Okay, I'll consider it. I already consider it almost every day. What else?"

"Promise me you won't do anything, *anything,* to interfere with Trixie and Sean's wedding."

He sighed. "I can't promise that."

Ellen dug her fingers into her seat cushion. "Then I don't promise not to write up what you've said! Maybe it'll be our feature article next month." She waved her hands as if displaying her next headline. *"What really happens behind closed doors..."*

Zach's head whipped around, his face pale. "You're a reporter?"

She lifted a shoulder. "Reporter, editor, layout, photographer. Sort of a Jill-of-all-trades for a small regional magazine in Portland. *Portland Today.*"

He dragged a hand down his face, muttering invectives. "I've heard of it."

Ellen perked up. "Really? You've heard of our magazine?"

"That surprises you?"

"Well, yeah. Considering how small our circulation currently is." She aimed a finger at him. "But we're growing. Our subscriptions grew by 26 percent last year." She gave a proud nod.

Zach's only response was a grunt and a furrowed brow as he stared out at the blowing snow and slick road.

She nudged his shoulder. "Lighten up, Zach. Your confession is safe with me. Our magazine's focus is tourism and economic growth in the Portland area, not exposing California state senators' dirty laundry."

"It was still careless of me to shoot off at the mouth like that. You never know who you could be talking to. I could have ruined..." He rubbed a spot near his heart, wincing, and exhaled deeply.

Ellen tipped her head. "You okay?"

"Ulcer. I'll be fine."

She shook her head. "Let me guess. The ulcer is stress-related?"

He sent her a silent, dark look.

"Zach, how can you stay in a job that is making you physically ill?"

"Plenty of people get stress-related ulcers."

"Plenty of unhappy, overworked people!"

He frowned and cast a glare at her. "What, your job doesn't stress you sometimes?"

"Not to the point of an ulcer. I love what I do. I look forward to going to the office each day. My job is fulfilling and exciting and new every day. I'm happy. Can you say the same?"

Zach popped a couple more antacids and crunched them without answering her. After a moment of tense quiet, she sighed. "Don't let the backstabbers and dirty dealers destroy your dreams for changing the world, Zach. Don't let your job suck all the joy from your life, and don't let misplaced loyalty keep you from pursuing a job that will make you happy." She wrapped her fingers around his wrist and squeezed. "You deserve to be happy."

When he glanced at her this time, his eyes held such sadness and longing that her heart contracted. She absorbed the wistfulness in his expression like a physical blow. Before she could say any more to encourage Zach, her cell phone trilled, jerking her out of the poignant moment. Reluctantly, she released his wrist and dug in her purse.

"Hello?" Ellen watched Zach's pensive expression as she poked a finger in one ear so she could hear over the static on the line.

"Where...you?...worried...this storm..." Trixie's broken words filtered through the bad connection, courtesy of the mountains.

"Trix, they closed the airport in Seattle. Zach Kallen and I are driving over together in a rental car." Ellen strained to hear her sister's response. Despite the garbled connection, she managed to relay the basics of the situation to her sister. "We could be late for the rehearsal. Don't wait for us. Stay on schedule, and we'll jump in when we get there. I'll call again with an update when I can, but cell towers will be few and far between until we get closer to Spokane."

"—kay." She heard the disappointment in her sister's voice, a reflection of her own frustration. "... careful...—ve you!"

"Love you, too." She keyed off the call and jammed the phone back in her handbag.

Turning on her seat to face Zach, Ellen chewed her bottom lip a moment, deciding what she should say regarding the emotional topic they'd broached before Trixie's call. "Zach, if you—"

"Why don't you try the radio?" he interrupted, his hard gaze telling her the previous subject was closed to debate. "See if you can get an update on the storm or road conditions east of here."

Fine. If he didn't want her support or encouragement, she'd keep it to herself. Even if his disillusionment and unhappiness did break her heart.

She mashed buttons on the radio until she found an all-talk, news station briefing listeners on the freak snowstorm mucking up Christmas travel for thousands of people in the Pacific Northwest.

"Sea-Tac Airport canceled all flights earlier this afternoon," the announcer droned. "And the area near the airport was one of the first to lose power. Reports of spotty outages continue to come into our station. But as this next wave of sleet and snow hits Seattle and temperatures drop after dark, a city-wide blackout is expected."

Ellen groaned and sent Zach a dismayed looked. "Next wave? There's more coming?"

He pulled a face and nodded. "Apparently. Just makes it all the more important we make tracks and get over the Cascades ahead of the front."

Ellen turned up the volume as the announcer said, "When sleet collects on trees and power lines, the weight of the ice brings down limbs and takes out power lines. Power company officials say it could take days to get the lights back on for everyone, and they warn people to stay away from downed power lines."

As if to punctuate the message, a large branch snapped free from a tree on the hillside ahead of them, starting a cascade of snow avalanching toward the highway. The cars in front of them swerved to avoid the encroaching snow pile and one small car spun completely around. Ellen gasped and clutched the dashboard. Zach, amazingly, remained calm and skillfully maneuvered around the skidding vehicle without incident.

At least their conversation about Zach's job woes and disillusionment had distracted her from the tedious and treacherous road conditions for a while. Now she gripped her seat belt strap and gnawed her bottom lip while she watched one car after another slip and slide on the icy interstate. Each time their rental car lost purchase, Ellen's adrenaline spiked, and she held her breath.

Driving well below the speed limit, they navigated past car after car that had slid off the road and gotten stuck in the drifts of snow at the side of the road. Finally, more than an hour later, they'd made it through Snoqualmie Pass. As they headed down the eastern side of the mountain, the radio announced that the state police were closing the mountainous section of highway through Snoqualmie Pass.

"That was close." Ellen blew out a sigh of relief. "If we hadn't made it through—"

A warm hand wrapped around her arm, and she lifted a curious gaze to Zach. His smile was confident and a tad smug. "I told you I'm gonna get you to Spokane in time for your sister's wedding. Have a little faith."

"It's not you I don't trust. These roads—" She motioned out the front window and shuddered.

His thumb stroked her wrist, stirring a heady tingle that skittered over her skin.

"Relax. I promise to take care of you." Giving her arm a final squeeze, he returned his hand to the steering wheel.

"Relax? Right. Easier said than done." While she wanted Zach to use both hands on the wheel for safety, she regretted the loss of his calming touch, the warmth of his fingers. She shook the tension from her arms and shoulders, rocking her head from side to side to loosen the tension screwing her muscles into knots.

"WDOT will close Interstate 90 near Moses Lake by nightfall, as temperatures are forecasted to drop—"

Zach snapped the radio off with a huff. "What possessed Sean and Trixie to choose Christmas weekend to get married?"

"Christmas is a beautiful time of year to marry! The church is all decorated with evergreen, poinsettias and lights, and all the family is already gathering for the holiday...."

Zach turned up a palm on the steering wheel matter-of-factly. "But they had to know they were gambling on weather conditions."

She grunted. "Like they were supposed to know the worst storm in twenty years would hit the weekend of their wedding."

"Maybe it's an omen. Maybe fate doesn't want them to marry."

Ellen crossed her arms over her chest and cast Zach a churlish scowl, ready to lambast him. Instead she saw the corner of his mouth twitch.

When he cut a furtive glance toward her, his grin broadened. She snorted and shook her head. "You're just yanking my chain, you butt!"

He chuckled. "Butt? Is that the best you can do?"

"Oh, you want me to be more creative? I have more colorful terms if you wish."

"Lay 'em on me." The twinkle of mischief in his eyes took the wind from her sail. The handsome scamp even had a dimple in his right cheek as he grinned at her.

She raised her chin. "No."

"Anyone ever tell you you're beautiful when you're mad?"

Ellen nearly choked. "What?"

"Yeah. Your cheeks flush, and your eyes light up, and your lips get pouty." He lifted his eyebrows and gave a tight nod. "Whew. Definitely hot."

Ellen could only goggle at him. Was she supposed to take him seriously? Could she take anything he'd said seriously? She turned back toward the passenger window, her thoughts spinning, and stared out at the ice and snow piled along the side of the road. Zach was probably just trying to distracted her from her worry over the road, over missing the wedding. That had to be it. Men like Zach never gave her a second look. Especially not when Trix was around. Her sister was a knockout. Ellen had always considered herself fairly ordinary. So was Zach's compliment just a line to calm her jitters over the icy roads?

Glancing over her shoulder, she narrowed a curious gaze on him. "You're a tough guy to figure out, Zach Kallen."

In return, he gave her an impish grin and a wink. "Thank you."

A few miles later, Ellen was lost deep in her own thoughts when Zach pulled off the interstate to get on a smaller state road.

Ellen twisted around in her seat, watching I-90 disappear behind them, along with the last daylight. "Where are you going?"

"Spokane, last time I checked."

"But—"

"You heard the radio guy. DOT is closing the interstate left and right. We're bound to get snagged in traffic or stuck at a barricade eventually. I've driven this highway before. It's a good alternative and appears to have been cleared by the road crews."

In the deepening gray of twilight, she surveyed the two-lane highway confirming his assessment. "Well, maybe here it has. But what about twenty miles down the road? The sun's going down, and you're taking a gamble, counting on getting through on a state road, Zach."

"A calculated risk, yes. But getting through on I-90 is iffy at this point, too."

Ellen twisted her lips, then opening the glove box, took out the road map provided by the rental agency. She perused the grid of roads checking the route he'd choosen. "If we go this way, where do you plan to reconnect with I-90?"

Zach tugged the map closer and, dividing his attention between the map and the road, he slid a finger along a red line indicating the highway they were on. "This section of road usually gets cleared because of travel between these towns. If we stay on until—"

A movement at the edge of the road distracted Ellen.
Deer. Several of them.
And they chose that moment to bolt in front of the car.
"Zach! Look out!"

Chapter 4

Zach jerked the wheel, stood on the brake. *Mistake.*

He missed the deer but felt the tires lock and slide. Nerves jumping, he steered into the skid. Still the car skated over the fresh glazing of ice. Too little, too late. Momentum carried the Malibu toward the steep drop at the side of the road.

Ellen screamed.

Zach's breath caught.

Packed ice and snow at the edge of the road served as a ramp, lofting them airborne for a instant. As they careened over the embankment, the hood of the car pitched forward. Sank.

Instinctively, he flung his arm across Ellen's chest, a futile attempt to brace her, protect her from the impact as the car landed. With a jarring crunch of metal, the passenger side of the car plowed into the deep drift of snow. Zach's head snapped right then left, smacking hard against his window. His shoulder belt dug into his collarbone as inertia pitched him sideways again. The Malibu spun another ninety degrees and sank farther into the snowdrift. Finally the car came to rest at an awkward angle on the icy hillside.

In the stunned silence, he exhaled sharply. Tasted blood. Heard the tremulous shudder of Ellen's frightened gasp.

For a moment, neither of them moved nor spoke. Finally he shook of the surreal sense of shock. His voice low and rough, he asked, "Are you okay?"

Cutting a wide-eyed glance toward him, she nodded, then wrinkled her brow. "You're bleeding."

He touched his mouth. "I think I bit my tongue."

"No." She reached for him, her hand shaking. "Your head." Gently, she probed his temple, parting his hair with her fingers. The delicate scent of her shampoo teased his nose as she leaned close, stretched across him to examine his forehead. His focus narrowed on the concerned pout of her lips, until she touched an especially sore spot on his scalp.

He sucked in a hiss of pain and caught her hand. Blood smeared her fingertips.

"Sorry. I—" Her gaze found his and held.

The warmth and concern swirling in her evergreen eyes burrowed to his marrow. Zach's pulse kicked into overdrive. Filling his lungs with a slow deep breath, he battled down the urge to have a second sample of her raspberry lips. Now was hardly the time to be distracted by a sexy mouth and bedroom eyes—post-crash adrenaline high or not.

"You have a cut. And it's swelling up a little." Her voice trembled as she eased back into her seat.

"I'll be all right." He tested the wound with his own fingers, and his head throbbed in protest. His head wound would wait. He had to get them back on the road...if possible.

He surveyed the position of the car, the steep grade of the icy embankment they'd gone over, and the depth of the snow at their doors, and his gut tightened. Chances were they'd be going nowhere fast.

Sending up a silent prayer, Zach shifted into Reverse and

gave the engine a little gas. The tires spun, but the car didn't budge. He tried again with the same results.

Ellen chewed her bottom lip and sent him an anxious look. "Can we push it out?"

"Worth a shot. You slide behind the wheel and gun the engine when I tell you to." Yanking the handle, he shouldered the door. Nothing.

He shoved again harder, trying to plow the impeding snow out of the way. But the weight of the slushy snow and ice pinned the door closed. The frozen blockade rose even higher on Ellen's side of the car. Zach groaned and turned toward her.

"We're trapped in here, aren't we?" she guessed, before he could deliver the bad news.

"We can probably climb out the window, but considering the height of the drift we're in, I doubt the two of us can get the car back on the road. We'll need a tow truck for that."

She nibbled her lip but kept a cool head. Either she hadn't played out the scenario and reached the conclusions he had, or she was much calmer under fire than he'd have expected. He cut the engine and sank back into his seat.

Ellen gave a tight nod, then lifted her purse to her lap and pulled out her cell phone. She studied the small screen, moved the phone higher, left, right...and sighed.

"No signal. Not even one bar." With a scowl, she flipped the phone closed and tossed it back in her bag. "What about yours?"

"I'll check." He turned and snagged his backpack, wincing when the movement sent a lightning bolt of pain through his skull. He pressed his palm against his temple.

"You should hold something against the cut to stop the bleeding." Ellen dug through her purse again. "Dang it. I don't even have a tissue in here."

Zach pulled an undershirt from his pack along with his cell. After handing her his phone to try, he rolled the shirt and held it to his head. Leaning the seat back, he closed his eyes. He needed to think, plan, figure out their next move.

Instead he replayed the rapid-fire seconds of the accident in his mind. Analyzing. Second-guessing. Jerking the wheel had been his first mistake given the conditions. Stomping the brake his second. He'd known better, but knee-jerk reaction had taken over when he'd seen the deer.

He squeezed his eyes tighter as stabbing guilt joined the throb of his head. The wreck was his fault. And because he'd forgotten basic winter driving skills, they were now stranded in the middle of nowhere during the worst storm in years.

The telltale beeps and musical tones of his cell broke the silence as Ellen tried to call for help. He heard her heavy sigh. Heard his phone snapped closed.

"Nothing. Zilch. We can't get a call out." The first hints of real worry quivered in her voice. "If we can't call for help and we can't push the car out…" She drew a ragged breath. "What do we do? Can we walk to a house to call?"

Zach pivoted on the seat to face her, steeling himself before breaking the bad news to her. "I think our best move is to stay put. It's getting dark and walking the side of the road would be dangerous. We don't know how far the closest house is and the temperature is already dropping. In the morning, we'll climb up to the road and—"

"In the morning!" In the fading daylight, he watched her eyes round with dismay. "You mean, spend the night here? In the car? In the cold?"

He clenched his teeth, wishing they had another solution. "Unless you have a better idea. I don't like it any more than you do, but I think staying with the car and waiting for help in the morning is the safest, smartest option."

The sparkle of tears pooled in her eyes, sucker punching him in the gut. "But—"

He reached for her, stroking a hand along her jaw, plowing his fingers into her hair. He cradled her head and rubbed the fluttering pulse in her neck with his thumb. "Hey, we're going to be all right. I'm not going to let anything happen to you."

Covering his hand with hers, she blinked back her tears and nodded. "I know. I'm sorry. I just—"

Nudging her chin up, he drilled his gaze on hers. "Ellen, I will get you to your sister's wedding tomorrow. Somehow, someway. I promise." He wasn't sure how he would keep that pledge, but the gratitude and relief reflected in her eyes spread a honeyed warmth through his blood.

Ellen squared her shoulders and tugged up a corner of her mouth. "And I promise not to fall apart on you. Even if this day does seems to keep going from bad to worse." She took the undershirt from him and dabbed it against his forehead. "I'm worried about that cut. You could have a concussion."

He shrugged, playing down the fiery ache pulsing under his skull. "Naw. Just a goose egg. I got worse knocks playing hockey in high school."

She pressed her mouth in a taut worried line. "Just the same, I think you should stay awake tonight. Just in case."

When she leaned closer to check the bleeding from the gash on his head, he tucked a wisp of her hair behind her ear. "I read that's a myth. I won't slip into a coma if I doze off later."

She arched an eyebrow. "Maybe. But do you really want to take the chance?"

"If I don't sleep, will you stay awake with me? Keep me company?" he murmured, his tone low and thick.

Ellen's breath hitched. Her gaze locked with his, then shifted to his lips. Her pupils grew, a clear signal of her body's response to him. "Uh—of course."

Clearing her throat, she leaned back and glanced away. Fidgeted.

So she was rattled by the crackle of chemistry between them, huh?

Memories of his strategic kiss in the parking garage revived the thrum of desire in his blood and sent a flash of heat through him. He could think of several ways to pass the hours of the night and also stave off the outside chill.

Rallying herself, Ellen rolled down her window and scooped a handful of snow.

Zach shivered as a blast of icy air filled the car.

"One thing I know isn't a myth is that you need ice to reduce the swelling of that bump." After wrapping his undershirt around the snowball, she pressed the homemade ice pack to his head.

He took the cold compress from her. "I can do that."

She closed the window and huddled deeper into her coat, while he searched for a way to make their predicament easier for her.

"If you're hungry, I have some crackers and a candy bar in my backpack."

She peeked out from the knit scarf she'd pulled up over her nose. "Thanks. Not now. But could we turn the heat back on?"

Zach hesitated. "I don't think we have enough gas to run the engine all night. We'll need to use the heater in spurts once it gets colder tonight."

"Oh." Her brow puckered, and she tipped her head to look out at the darkening sky. She chuckled softly, without any real humor in her tone. "What a way to spend the first night of the Christmas weekend." She glanced at him and mustered a brave smile. "At least it'll be a wild story to tell our kids at family gatherings in years to come, huh?"

He arched an eyebrow, and a deep blush darkened the pink already staining her cheeks from the cold.

"I—I don't mean *our* kids." She waved a hand between them and shook her head. "I meant each of our kids. Separately." She paused again. "Um, not that there's anything wrong with having kids with you. I…I mean—I don't think… We don't…I'm not—"

Amused by her backpedaling, he cocked his head and pulled his mouth into a lopsided grin.

She huffed in disgusted and embarrassment. "I'm going to shut up now."

She squeezed her eyes closed and slumped down in the seat.

"Santa is going to hear about this. That's for sure."

Wrinkling her nose, she glanced over at him. "Santa?"

He nodded and waved a hand toward the windshield. "We were run off the road by eight reindeer."

Ellen snorted. "Those were whitetails, not reindeer."

He crossed his arms over his chest. "Oh, they'll be reindeer when I tell people about this."

Her musical laughter sang through the car, stirring a different sort of warmth deep inside him.

"It's the night before Christmas Eve. Do you know where your reindeer are?" she asked in a deep voice.

His smile grew. "I'm sure at least one of hooligans had a red nose. Yep, Santa is definitely going to get a sternly worded letter from me."

Ellen grabbed his arm and lowered her tone to a conspiratorial whisper. "Hey, do you think we can blackmail Santa and get more loot out of this? I've been wanting a new car for a while now. Maybe this is the year to ask for a shiny black Mustang. Hmm?"

Zach chuckled. "Now you're talkin'. But why stop at a Mustang? Go for something European and sporty. You'd look good in a Porsche Boxster."

She tipped her head and nodded. "You think? Okay. Porsche it is." Humor laced her tone, and the fading daylight couldn't hide the sparkle of amusement in her eyes.

Zach was struck by how her face glowed when she smiled, how beautiful she looked with the nip of cold staining her cheeks. His heart performed a tuck and roll in his chest. The urge to kiss her slammed into him, stealing his breath. He'd never been so wildly attracted to a woman before, and the intensity of his response to her laughter and her kiss rocked him to his core.

His face must have reflected the change in his mood, because she knitted her brow again and gave him a puzzled look. "Zach, what's wrong?"

He shook his head and turned his gaze out the driver's side window. "Nothing. Forget it."

He sighed restlessly, and when his breath fogged the glass, his mind flashed to an image of two bodies tangled together, steaming up the windows in earnest. Zach swallowed a groan.

The snowball ice pack she'd made him had melted into a

drippy mess. He chucked the wet undershirt into the backseat, then dug in his backpack. "I think I'm ready for some of those crackers."

More than he wanted food, he wanted a distraction from the tantalizing ideas that now tickled his brain. Somehow he knew Ellen wasn't the sort of woman who'd entertain the notion of a fling simply because it was convenient to their circumstances. Especially since he intended to spoil all her sister's best-laid wedding plans.

Guilt bit hard on his conscience. He'd tried to talk to Sean about his misgivings concerning the wedding months ago, and Sean hadn't taken him seriously. Anytime he'd raised the subject since then, something or someone—usually Trixie—had interrupted their conversation and derailed the topic. Now he faced the unpleasant task of disrupting a celebration months in the making. And wouldn't *that* make him the life of the party?

But Zach just couldn't believe that Sean "Girl in Every Port" O'Banion had chosen marriage over womanizing of his own free will. Sean had been a hound dog all through college and earned a reputation in their fraternity as the least likely to settle down before forty.

Zach fished out a pack of cheese and peanut butter crackers, then shifted uncomfortably on the seat. Being a wedding saboteur was never his goal, but wasn't sparing his friend from the train wreck of a broken marriage the most important consideration? He had an obligation to be forthright with his best friend, even if he hated spoiling the festivities, putting a fly in the proverbial punch bowl—disappointing Ellen...

Zach frowned. When had Ellen become a factor in his plans?

"So tell me some of your family's Christmas traditions."

He jerked his head toward Ellen when she spoke...and regretted it when a bolt of pain shot through his skull. He gritted his teeth and leaned his head against the seat back. "Don't really have any."

"Aw, come on. There must be something you like to do every Christmas? Caroling? Eggnog at midnight? Waking at dawn to open all your gifts?" Night had swallowed the car in darkness now. Only the thin glow of the moon filtering through the dissipating clouds provided any light.

Zach tapped the dimmer switch to turn on the car's interior lights, then shrugged. "The last two Christmases I've spent alone at my apartment, watching whatever pro football game was on and eating the dry fruitcake my mom insists on sending every year." He grunted. "I hate fruitcake."

"Alone? That's awful!"

Her tone vibrated with a sympathy and compassion that pricked like unwanted pity, yet also touched a vulnerable place inside him he hated to acknowledge—the lonely part of him that dreaded the upcoming holiday.

Zach shoved the uneasy duality down, hiding his vulnerability on this point with humor. "No, my mom's fruitcake is what's awful. But I think it makes her feel less guilty about missing every holiday with me. See, she has a tradition of taking a trip somewhere tropical every year with the current boyfriend. This year it's Hawaii."

Ellen harrumphed and crossed her arms over her chest as if she were the offended party. "You shouldn't be alone on Christmas. That's just not right."

Zach shrugged. "No big deal."

She clutched at his arm again, leaned toward him. "Come to my parents' house. Spend Christmas with us. I know they won't mind. We always have extra folks around during the holidays. Exchange students who couldn't afford to fly home, neighbors who live far from family…the more the merrier. Trixie will be off on her honeymoon so you can stay in her room. What do you say?"

"I don't know. Your family doesn't know me."

"But Sean does. And he'll be family by then, so…"

Zach grunted, biting back his argument that Sean might not be family…if Zach had a chance to talk to him before the wedding. And if his voice of caution *did* change the groom's mind, Zach would most certainly be persona non grata at the bride's house.

Ellen's face darkened, telling him she understood his grunt. Aiming a finger at him, she shook her head. "I'm warning you. If you try to mess things up for Sean and Trixie—"

He caught her finger in his hand. "The point isn't to mess things up. I'm not some kind of spiteful monster who enjoys disrupting weddings. I don't even want to come between Sean and Trixie."

"Good!"

"But—"

Ellen growled and yanked her finger from his grasp. "But nothing!"

As much as he hated explaining himself, Ellen clearly needed a little context. "Do you know how many girls Sean dated in college?"

She hesitated, frowned. "No. Why does that matter?"

"It matters, because he once told me he pitied men who tied themselves down to one woman before turning forty. He dated a different girl virtually every weekend throughout college."

Lifting an eyebrow, she tipped her head at a skeptical angle.

"No lie. Our junior year alone, he went out with twenty-five different women. Does that sound to you like a guy who is ready to settle down and play happy home with one woman?"

Ellen's brow dipped, and her eyes narrowed. "Twenty-five?"

"Just during our junior year. He slowed up a bit our senior year, because he was busy with his final project and term papers. He was a hound dog, but he was also studious."

Scowling, Ellen snuggled deeper into her coat. "I don't believe you. And even if it is true, it's a moot point. He's changed. He's in love with Trixie, and they are happy. Let bygones be bygones, and let them get married in peace." Her eyes beseeched him, tugging at a soft spot inside him. "Please?"

Zach dragged a hand down his face and groaned. "I have to be sure my friend is doing the right thing. I have to speak up if there's even a chance he's got qualms or doubts about this wedding. The Sean I knew in college would not be marrying someone he's known for only a year. He wouldn't be marrying, period."

She brooded for a moment, staring into the blackness out the window. Then, pinning him with a challenging gaze, she raised her chin. "Fine. Do what you feel you must. But Sean will still marry my sister. I know he will. Their love will prevail, and they'll have a long, happy life together. You'll see." She gave him a smug grin and tugged her scarf back up around her cheeks.

Her sanguinity shone in her eyes as she settled back in her seat, wearing a self-assured smile. "And you're still invited for Christmas. Jaded agenda or not, no one should be alone at Christmas. Who knows? Maybe after spending a little time around a family where love works the way it should and couples stay together for the long haul, we might even change your dim view of the state of marriage in America."

Her confident optimism sparked a hopefulness deep inside Zach he hadn't known in years. Maybe his willingness to buy into her happily-ever-after scenario was nothing but a product of holiday sentimentality, but he savored the ribbon of warmth that unfurled in his chest. Pulling his mouth in a lopsided grin, he turned the interior light off to conserve the car's battery. "I hope you're right, sweetheart."

Chapter 5

Ellen pushed the light button on her watch and squinted at the glowing display. 10:28 p.m. By her calculation, they'd been sitting in this freezing car for five hours now, give or take a few minutes. Her cramping leg muscles and sore butt said they'd been cooped up more like fifty hours, and her icy nose and fingers agreed.

She stretched her back as best she could and shook the ache from her legs to keep the blood flowing. Glancing at Zach, who'd been suspiciously quiet for the last several minutes, she gave his shoulder a nudge. "Hey, you're not falling asleep on me, are you?"

"Maybe," he mumbled. "I've been up since 4:00 a.m. to catch my flight outta Sacramento, and only had three hours' sleep the night before that. Dosing off is definitely a possibility."

"How's your head?"

"Still attached to my neck."

"Har, har. Does it hurt much?"

"Define *much*?"

In the deep blackness of the night, their conversations over the past several hours had been a bit like listening to a talk-radio station. Faceless voices exchanging banter. And confidences. Ellen had often wondered how people could call talk-radio shows and spill their guts to a stranger—for public broadcast. But after five hours—give or take a few minutes—of passing time with Zach, trying not to think about the cold when her nose and feet were almost numb, she had more sympathy for the loquacious callers. Anonymity—or in her case, the complete darkness—bred openness. Confiding in someone was easier if you didn't have to look them in the eye, see their reaction, feel the weight of their gaze.

She gnawed her bottom lip, remembering just *how* honest she'd been with Zach. Had she really admitted to all the embarrassing things she and her girlfriends had done last year in New Orleans during Mardi Gras? Operating under the influence of a couple Hurricanes from Pat O'Brien's Pub was no excuse for lifting her shirt for perfect strangers.

At least he'd confessed a few of his embarrassing moments when his turn came, and they'd laughed together over the verbal picture he painted of his "worst Halloween costume idea ever." However, remembering her admission of how she'd lost her virginity at summer camp made Ellen cringe. She'd crossed the line there. Zach's awkward response and hasty change of subject spoke volumes. She shuddered.

"I agree," Zach said, jolting her from her uncomfortable reminiscing.

"What?" Ellen's heart tripped. Lord, if she'd said something aloud by accident and giving away the track of her thoughts—

"You shivered. And I agree that it's past time to crank the heat. I can't feel my ears anymore."

She heard him fumbling, then the car engine rumbled to life. Soon heated air poured out of the vents, and she rubbed her hands in front of the warm stream.

"There's an Italian restaurant in Sacramento," he said without preamble, "that has the best eggplant parmesan on the planet."

"I don't like eggplant. Too squishy."

"No way. It's awesome. I'd kill for a plate of that stuff right now." He chuckled. "In fact, I'd settle for my mom's fruitcake at this point. I'm starving. Those crackers didn't go far."

"Thanks for sharing them with me. We wouldn't have even had that much if it were left up to me." She paused. "Oh, wait…I think I have a breath mint if you want it."

He chuckled. "A breath mint?"

"Better than nothing."

"Barely. But what the hell. Yes, please, I'd like a breath mint before I start chewing on my shoelaces."

She laughed at the image of Zach gnawing on his foot and dug blindly in her purse until she found the candy. After popping one in her mouth, she found his hand in the dark. "Here. Take the rest of the roll. Merry Christmas."

"Gee, and I didn't get you anything."

Ellen leaned her head back and closed her eyes, savoring the warm air from the heater and enjoying the easy repartee she'd found with Zach. His sense of humor helped her keep her mind off their situation and the cold night.

"Say, if you like Italian food, I'll have to have my mom make her homemade lasagna for you the day after Christmas. Oh, man. Talk about good!"

They tortured themselves for the next several minutes discussing favorite foods and restaurants, until the pinch of hunger in Ellen's gut morphed into unexplained nausea. Surely the breath mint couldn't have made her sick. She tried to ignore the queasiness, but the sickness only grew.

"Can we not talk about food anymore? I don't feel so good."

Zach clicked on the interior light, and they both blinked as their eyes adjusted to the relative brightness.

"What's wrong?" A wrinkle of worry dented his forehead.

"I'm just feeling kinda sick to my stomach." She shrugged, finding her shoulder sore and stiff from banging the car door when they crashed. "I'm sure it's nothing."

"Can I do anything? Do you want a couple of my antacids?"

He pulled the roll of chewable tablets from his pocket and extended them to her.

She shook her head, but cataloged his compassion and concern with the other reasons for her growing fondness for her travel companion—his determination to play havoc with Trix's wedding aside.

Zach stashed his roll of heartburn remedy and leaned his head back. As she visually checked the swelling of the knot on his head, he winced and pinched the bridge of his nose. She had a bottle of ibuprofen—in her suitcase, which was probably still stuck in the powerless Sea-Tac terminal. She sighed. The painkiller was no use to them there.

"I wonder if this storm has taken out the power in Spok—" She yawned and fought to keep her increasingly heavy eyelids open. "Excuse me. In Spokane."

Zach reached for the dimmer switch. "Want me to turn the light out so you can nap?"

"No, I…I'm going to stay awake with you, remember?"

"Nonsense. I don't need you to babysit me." His churlish tone startled her. "Go to sleep if you want. I'll be fine."

When Zach turned off the light again, Ellen shivered. "Somehow the car feels colder in the dark."

"It's not."

"I know it isn't *really*. I said it *seems* that way." Under her breath she added, "Grump."

Ellen closed her eyes and took a deep, slow breath trying to soothe the seesawing in her stomach. She absolutely would not toss her cookies in front of Zach. Talk about embarrassing. Geez, what if she'd caught a stomach virus? That would make for a miserable wedding for her.

"I've been waiting for weeks for the caviar Trixie ordered for the reception. If I'm sick, I may not get any."

"What?" Zach sounded groggy, confused.

She supposed her comment did sort of come from left field.

"Nothing. Never mind." The thought of food made her queasier. She needed a distraction. She tried to think of a safe topic of conversation, but the warmth blasting from the heater made her all the sleepier. Her head felt too fuzzy to think.

But she had to keep Zach awake. Zach, who was coming for Christmas…

"You won't have a stocking. We need to get you a stocking." She fought down a wave of nausea and blinked hard to stay alert. "Santa owes us." She scowled, and her head swam dizzily. She closed her eyes…just for a minute. "His reindeer did this. Bad reindeer."

"That was a joke. There is no Santa. Never was."

"You're a Scrooge, Zach Kallen. Where's your Christmas spirit?"

"I left it back in Seattle, 'bout the time the power failed."

"Kallen the Scrooge…" she grumbled, then yawned again. "I don't want to talk to you if you're gonna be mean."

"Good! My head hurts too much to talk anyway."

Ellen folded her arms over her chest and pouted. "I didn't ask to be stranded with you. They closed the airport, you know. How am I supposed to get to my wedding?"

"Sean's wedding, not yours."

"I know!"

"Do you mind? I asked you to be quiet." His tone had become surlier.

Grouch. Why had she agreed to travel with that grump? She'd get to the wedding on her own! 'Cept the airport was snowed in.

She rested her head against the cold window. She never could sleep sitting up. Cars, planes… She was going to be late for the wedding. She and Zach Kallen would miss it….

"Hey, I just thought of something," she mumbled groggily. "When I marry you, my name will be Ellen Kellen." She giggled, and her eyelids drooped.

"It's *Kallen,* with an *A.* And who said we were getting married?"

Opening her eyes seemed a struggle. "That's where we're going now, dummy!" She frowned and rubbed her temples. "If this stupid plane would ever take off."

Zach gritted his teeth. Her crazy rambling was making his head ache worse. "Go to sleep, Ellen. You're not making any sense."

When she didn't answer, he clicked on the light again and glanced her way. Her eyes were finally closed, her chest rising and falling in the steady rhythm of sleep. Thank goodness. He wasn't sure how much more of her babbling he could take. Normally he considered himself a pretty tolerant guy, but in the last few minutes, Ellen's drowsy chatter had become exponentially more irritating.

Now, he studied her fragile features as she slept. Her dark lashes fanned against her pale skin, her bowed lips slightly pursed and maddeningly kissable. Like a ripe raspberry…

He paused and frowned. Her lips were no longer the sweet dark pink hue that made him conjure images of berries. Her lips were dark cherry red, and her fingernails had a bluish tint.

Not good. Why…?

Zach struggled to clear the hazy fog from his brain. Where had he heard about this? Was it a bill he was working on with the senator? An article he'd read?

Fuzzy details drifted through his pain and sleep muddled mind. A public service announcement the senator had been featured in…dangers in the home…faulty heaters…

The heater. Exhaust. Engine running…

Understanding slapped him like an icicle to the heart.

Adrenaline snapped him to alertness.

Snow must have clogged the tail pipe, sending carbon monoxide into the car with them. Drowsiness, headache, nausea, even his own irritability could be explained by the oxygen-depleted air they'd been breathing. By running the engine to stay warm, he could have killed them both. He'd unwittingly turned their shelter into a death trap.

"Dammit!" He cut the engine with a vicious twist and leaned over the center console toward Ellen. "Ellen?"

She slumped against the passenger door, her head lolling to one side. Fear squeezed his chest. What if he was too late?

Clenching his teeth, he battled down the negative thought. *Do something!*

He had to get her outside, get her into the fresh air, get her to breathe oxygen before the carbon monoxide could do more damage.

"Ellen, wake up!" He slapped her cheeks, shook her shoulders, desperate to rouse her. "Come on, sweetheart. No napping right now."

When she still didn't respond, panic gripped his gut. Ellen was smaller than he was, and the lack of oxygen could have taken a far harsher toll on her. "Ellen!"

Zach clambered into the backseat and tried to open the door, jamming his shoulder into the immoveable blockade. The deep snowdrift they'd sunk into and the icy temperatures had the doors sealed tight. Plan B was the window. He'd get her out of the car one way or another. He had to.

Or she'd die.

Chapter 6

Having fought the frozen window down, Zach pulled Ellen's limp body through the gap between the front seats into the back. Holding her under her arms, he awkwardly turned and maneuvered his feet out the window first. After kicking snow out of the way and packing it into a firm shelf with his legs, he rolled to his stomach, positioning himself to drag Ellen through the small opening.

Bitter winds lashed them as the promised cold front moved in. Despite the arctic chill, he yanked off his jacket and spread it across the snow as a layer of protection between her and the icy bed of snow. Again he patted her cheeks, trying to wake her. "Ellen! Please, honey, open your eyes."

With a groan, a wrinkled brow, and a hard shiver, she peered up at him through narrow slits. "Go away. I feel like crud, and I just wanna sleep."

He expelled a sigh of relief when she roused, his breath clouding in front of him and the bubble of panic in his chest easing its grip. "You feel like crud, because we were inhaling exhaust."

He shook her shoulder when she closed her eyes again and turned, burrowing her head deeper into the folds of his jacket.

"You need to stay awake until I'm sure you've gotten the bad stuff out of your body and replaced it with good oxygen."

She moaned a protest, then raised unfocused eyes to his. "Your coat smells good. Like summer. Pine and…hmm, sunshine." She lifted a corner of her mouth groggily. "And sex."

He barked a startled laugh. "Sex? I promise you, I haven't been wearing my coat during sex."

Although now that she mentioned it, the idea had merit. Nothing like a little body friction to build heat.

She hummed drowsily in response, the low rumbling sound conjuring images for Zach of the topic she'd raised—images of Ellen's body nestled against his. Naked. Sweaty. Arching into him. Would she make that low rumbling purring in the throes of lovemaking? He huffed, irritated with himself. Now was neither the time nor the place to let himself get sidetracked by his libido. Even if she had brought the subject up.

"Can you sit up? Take a few deep breaths? We gotta get some O two circulating in your blood."

"Blood?" She wobbled to a seated position. "Am I bleeding?"

"No. No blood. You just need to breathe deeply. Get some fresh air."

She glanced around at their surroundings. "What happened? Where are we?"

Zach sighed and rubbed her arm to calm her. Confusion was another effect of carbon-monoxide poisoning. "We ran off the road. Remember? Santa's reindeer. We're stuck until someone finds us in the morning."

Please, God, let someone find them in the morning if not before. Without food or water, without heat, he doubted they could survive much longer than a day or two.

Zach chafed his arms and surveyed the isolated stretch of road where they'd gotten stuck. As the clouds were pushed westward by the encroaching cold front, the moon cast a bright glow over the wintery landscape. Evergreens burdened with snow and ice bent low to the ground and icicles tinkled in the crisp whip of the breeze.

"It's f-freezing out here. I want to get back in the car." Ellen tried to move past him, and he caught her around the waist.

"Not until the car airs out. Stay down behind the bank of snow, out of the wind."

Color slowly crept back into her complexion and her lips, and the anxiety tying Zach in knots loosened. If she'd died…

Gritting his teeth, he shoved the chilling thought of losing Ellen aside and focused on their survival. Tomorrow they'd have to do something to make the wrecked car more visible from the road. The white car blended into the backdrop of the snow too well. Surely the highway patrol would be out in force looking for stranded travelers. Wouldn't they?

Ellen hunched her shoulders and tucked her nose inside her scarf. Without the car's heater, the night's cold would be brutal. He surveyed the back end of the Malibu, estimating if he could scoop the snow away from the tailpipe. The back fender was sunk in about three feet of snow, meaning the tailpipe was closer to four-feet deep. Giving the snow a test scoop, he encountered a hard crusty layer of ice on the top. The plunge in temperatures had left the slushy snow frozen and impenetrable. Without tools other than his hand, it seemed unlikely he could dig the tailpipe clear enough to run the engine.

Tipping his head back, he gazed up at the plethora of stars that twinkled through the clearing clouds.

"I always wonder how many are up there."

He jerked his gaze back to Ellen when she spoke, surprised to hear her so alert and cognizant already. She, too, had her head tilted back admiring the night sky.

"Without the city lights, you can see so many stars." She hugged herself, and her teeth chattered.

In the pale wash of moonlight, the high cheekbones and soft lines of Ellen's face were cast in sharp relief. Snowflakes dusted the fringe of her scarf, and the wisps of her frosty breath swirled around her like confetti in a snow globe.

Nothing she could wear at the wedding tomorrow would make her any more lovely than she looked at that moment. He acknowledged the tug of emotion in his chest, even if indulging in sentimentality was rare for him. The scare she'd given him with her unresponsiveness, her skin so pale and her lips white, had shaken him. Shattered the illusion that the attraction and connection between himself and Ellen was no more than passing interest. She'd gotten under his skin in a way no other woman had.

With her golden hair lit by the moon, her cheeks rosy from the cold and the diamond glint of snowflakes clinging to her eyelashes, she reminded him of the winter fairies from his childhood bedtime stories. His mother used to read the magical tales to him on cold nights like tonight. The winter fairies were cousins of Jack Frost, his mom said. Enchanted pixies dusting the earth with glittering snow and sparkling ice.

He swallowed hard when a lump of nostalgia swelled in his throat. He and his mom had made some good memories, come through some tough times.

Ellen turned to him, caught him staring.

"Zach?" She cocked her head and gave him a peculiar look. "Where's your coat?"

"You're sitting on it."

"I'm wh—" She glanced down, seemed surprised to realize his jacket was her buffer to the snowbank.

Your coat smells good. He wondered how much of the time she'd been under the influence of the carbon monoxide she'd remember later.

Her gaze snapped up to his, wide with horror. "You must be freezing!"

Yeah, pretty much. He suppressed a shiver. "I'm all right."

"Why'd you let me hog your coat?" She scrambled to pull it from under her and hand it to him.

He shrugged and gratefully accepted his coat back. The

lining was still warm from her body heat. "I didn't want you lying in the snow after I pulled you out the window."

An incredulous look crumpled her brow, and she shook her head. "And they say chivalry is dead." She touched his arm, her eyes bright in the moonlight. "Zach, that has to be the sweetest thing anyone has ever done for me."

Her accolades left him off-balance. He'd only been doing what he thought was right. "Any guy would do the same. It's no big deal."

"It is to me." She leaned in and kissed his cheek. Her lips warmed his frozen cheek, and a tantalizing heat spread through his core when she met his gaze again.

He cleared his throat. "So…how are you feeling now?"

"Besides cold?" She flashed him a wry little smile that wrapped around his heart. "A lot better. Thanks to you." Her grin brightened as she took another cleansing breath, exhaling a puff of white fog. "I hate to think what could have happened if—"

He touched her lips to stop her. "But it didn't, and we're going to be fine. Let's not borrow trouble, huh?"

She chuckled. "Look at you being the positive one, the encourager. I thought that was my job."

He wiggled his eyebrows. "I'm full of surprises." Hitching his head toward the car window, he added, "Let's get out of this wind. I think the car is safe now."

With an enthusiastic nod, Ellen scooted across the packed snow and climbed through the back window of the Malibu. Zach followed her in then leaned forward and turned the key only long enough to roll the window up, leaving a crack for ventilation—just in case.

Neither of them bothered to climb back into the front seat, as if by mutual consent. In the dim light from the moon, Ellen sent him a lingering gaze and voiced his thoughts. "If we can't run the heater, then maybe…we should share body heat."

Zach's pulse kicked into high gear. "I—"

"Not, like, getting naked or that kind of extreme survivalist thing," she hurried to add, then glanced down at her hands.

Lifting the corner of his mouth, he chuckled. "I was actually about to suggest the same thing." He scrunched across the seat, and she stiffened when he put his hand on her coat sleeve. "Let me know if you change your mind about that getting naked part—" He grinned again when she whipped a shocked expression toward him. "—'Cause that kinda sounds like fun to me."

"Wh— Zach!" She gave him a nervous-sounding laugh but relaxed enough for him to nudge her forward on the seat. He slid in behind Ellen, pulled her onto his lap, and folded her snugly inside the lapels of his coat. She propped her feet on the seat and rested her head on his shoulder.

"Go to sleep if you want. Lord knows there's not much else to do," he said.

"We could sing Christmas carols."

"Pass."

She chuckled. "We could play I Spy."

He snorted. "No thanks."

He felt the vibration of her soft laugh against his chest, reverberating through him. Naked or not, the press of her body fueled a rush of heat through his veins.

"I know…" She flattened a hand over his heart and tipped her head back to look up into his face. A whimsical grin dimpled her cheek as she started to sing. "Ninety nine bottles of beer on the wall. Ninety-nine bottles of beer…"

Zach groan-laughed. "No!"

Ellen's smile brightened, her eyes twinkling with mischief in the moonlight. "If one of those bottles should happen to fall—"

Temptation overwhelmed him, and he caught her lips with his.

Ellen's eyes widened. Her body tensed. For a split second, he feared she'd bolt across the car, scrambling away from him.

Instead, she sighed into his mouth and plowed her fingers into his hair. When her lips parted, he deepened the kiss, tasting breath mints and pure bliss. Desire hummed through his body as their mouths meshed and their tongues dueled. She mewled softly, igniting his every nerve ending.

After a moment, when she ducked her head and sucked in

a deep breath, Zach fought down the surge of adrenaline pounding through him. Maybe he was rushing her. Maybe he was wrong about her intentions. He needed to give her space and time and—

"Or we could make out like teenagers in the backseat at a drive-in." Her breathless suggestion interrupted his recriminations.

She lifted her chin, grinning devilishly, and met his eyes with an expression that mirrored the fire blazing in his blood. Cradling the back of his head with one hand, she drew his mouth back down to hers.

Ellen's heart thumped a nervous cadence, unsure how Zach would react to her boldness. She'd surprised herself, tossing caution to the bitter northern wind to steal a few minutes of reckless passion with Zach. Normally she was so much more reserved, more patient in her relationships with men. But nothing about this situation was normal, and she sensed Zach wasn't like the men she usually dated. He had a raw honesty and depth of emotion that he tried to hide, but which she read in the intensity of his gaze. She felt an elemental connection to him that went beyond her profound physical attraction to him. If she'd believed in something as mystical as fate or destiny, she'd say this night, the storm, their being stranded was all part of a cosmic plan.

From deep in his throat, Zach growled his agreement to her suggestion and tucked her more firmly against his body. Holding her close, he slid down on the seat until she was lying on top of him. In the cramped confines of the backseat, he had to bend his knees, and Ellen straddled him, her legs folded under her. The position was awkward, but at the same time highly erotic. Her pulse kicked faster.

Zach's hands framed her face, and he captured her mouth again, nibbling at first then drawing harder, fuller kisses from her.

Angling her head to brush her lips along his jaw, Ellen savored the rough scrape of his unshaven chin.

"You're right. This is better than I Spy," she whispered, while skimming kisses across his cheek, moving toward his ear.

He finger-combed her hair behind her ear, providing himself access to the curve of her neck for hot, open-mouthed sampling. She sighed when he feathered his tongue over the throbbing pulse point, and she gasped when he bit gently on her earlobe. Pure pleasure skimmed through her veins as he teased the sensitive spot behind her ear...under her chin...at the hollow of her throat.

His hands skated down her back then up, under the hem of her coat and inside the edge of her sweater. When he settled his hands against her warm skin, she gasped and arched away from his touch.

He sent her a curious frown. "Ellen."

She smiled ruefully. "Your hands are cold."

He winced. "Sorry." He pulled his hands from under her clothing and rubbed them together briskly.

She caught his wrists, stopping him. "Allow me."

He held her gaze as she guided his hands under the front hem of her sweater and beneath her bra. His throat convulsed as he swallowed, and even in the dim light from the moon, she saw the fire that brightened his gaze. Her heart thrashed against her ribs as he cupped his hands over her breasts and gently molded them with his fingers.

Liquid heat pooled low in her belly, and a hum of pleasure vibrated in her throat. When he shifted his grasp so that his thumbs could abrade her nipples, an electric sensation coursed through her and almost made Ellen come undone. Arching her back, she strained to be closer, feel more of his body pressed to hers.

"More," she murmured as her mouth mated with his. Need flared hot and wild inside her, urging her on, obliterating the voice of caution. She'd almost died earlier tonight, yet when she kissed Zach, when he touched her, she never felt more alive.

Her body cried for him, longing to have him buried inside her, binding them. The power of the urge that drove her forward made no sense to her, went against everything she'd professed about relationships. But in the few short hours she'd known Zach, she'd experienced exhilarating joy and bone-chilling fear with him. Now, as he dipped his head and drew her peaked nipple into his mouth, she felt the most exquisite pleasure she'd ever known. Her skin flashed hot as he slid a hand up her thigh, under her skirt and inside the elastic of her panties.

His fingers stroked her nimbly, and Ellen angled her hips to provide better access. He sank one finger, then another, inside her, imitating the coupling her body craved. Closing her eyes and savoring the sweet friction, she saw spots of light dance before her. She mewled softly as the pulsing tension built inside her, until her every muscle was strung tight and her nerves crackled.

Finally, with a gasp, she plunged headlong into a maelstrom of sensation and a heated rush of pure bliss. She gripped his shoulders and cried Zach's name, bucking against his hand as her climax swept through her.

In the wake of her powerful release, he held her more tightly and their teeth clicked as she kissed him, trying to express physically the intensity of emotion that swamped her. She thrust her fingers into his hair and delved deeper with her tongue, her heart racing, her body quaking. He wrapped his arms around her, squeezing so tight it almost hurt. And still she couldn't get enough of him. Breathlessly, she clambered to wrap herself around him, lock herself more fully against his taut, lean frame.

"Zach—" she rasped, her hands fumbling with his belt, fighting to rid him of the cloth barrier that kept them from the union of bodies and souls.

A groan rumbled from his throat as he stilled her hands, bringing them to his lips. The muscles in his jaw bunched as he gritted his teeth. "Ellen, we have to stop. We… I don't have any protection with me."

She raised her head and blinked at him, her vision unfocused at first. For a moment, his words didn't register. All Ellen knew was the drumming of her heartbeat in her ears, the whirlwind of emotion that muddled her thoughts, the pounding hunger for some elusive something that only he could fulfill. But when he curled his fingers into her hair and drilled her with his laser-blue eyes, her breath caught. And his words clicked into place.

He was being responsible, cautious, pragmatic. He was protecting her. Yet every fiber of her heart and mind screamed in protest.

Ellen drew a ragged breath, tried to ignore the disappointment that lanced her chest. Nodding, she whispered, "You're right."

His grip tightened, pulling slightly at her hair as he narrowed a penetrating gaze on hers. "Believe me, there is nothing I want more right now than to make love to you. But…I won't do anything to hurt you. I have to…I have to do what's right."

After kissing her soundly, he tucked her head under his chin, and she nestled closer. Her body still shook with unspent desire, with adrenaline, from the cold, and he held her securely, warming her all the way to her core.

His word choice hadn't escaped her. *Make love.* They shared an unspoken agreement that what had just happened between them was more than meaningless sex to fill the empty hours. They'd both been driven by something deeper, something real, something new and amazing and powerful. Ellen's heart performed a slow roll in her chest.

She was falling in love with Zach.

Zach stared into the darkness, cradling Ellen against him, the thudding of her heart a steady cadence against his own drumming beat. His body thrummed with unsated longing, and his thoughts stirred restlessly.

He'd never wanted a woman the way he wanted Ellen—and not just for a quickie in the backseat of a rental car. He wanted more. He wanted to know her heart and spirit. He wanted more time with her than a whirlwind holiday wedding weekend.

When had he become the kind of guy to get emotionally entangled with a woman? He wasn't sure. Yet sometime between his impulsive kiss in the parking garage and the sound of his name on her lips as she shattered in his arms, he'd lost his heart to Ellen.

So now what did he do? How had his life become so complicated?

He stroked her back when she shivered and checked his watch in the light from the moon. Almost 2:00 a.m. The longest, coldest hours of the night still lay ahead. Tipping his face toward the window, he glanced up at the night sky to check the weather conditions.

And the sight that greeted him stole his breath.

Chapter 7

"Oh, man. Ellen, look!"

Ellen's pulse jumped, uncertain how to interpret the fevered pitch in Zach's tone. Muscles tensing and mentally bracing for another tragic turn to their dilemma, Ellen shifted on the seat and leaned across Zach to glance up at the stars.

A swirling greenish-blue and yellow glow twisted and writhed over the treetops, casting an eerie light across the snow. Ellen stared, awestruck for a few staggering heartbeats before what she was seeing clicked in her brain. "Oh my God. Are those the Northern Lights?"

"I'd say so. Pretty impressive, huh?"

Ellen angled her head to meet Zach's eyes, a fresh, excitement-borne burst of adrenaline coursing through her.

A smile tugged the corner of his mouth. "Want to go outside for a better view of nature's show?"

She returned a playful smile. "Darn right. Race you!"

Zach smacked a kiss on her lips, and she tumbled backward

as he sat up. With a squawk and a laugh, Ellen scrambled to roll down the window again and slide out onto the packed snow.

A frigid blast of air buffeted her as she hoisted herself from the car, and she almost changed her mind about the outdoor viewing. Snuggling with Zach in the protection of the car had been awfully nice. The circle of his arms had been secure, his body warm, his kisses sweet—so sweet that she'd forgotten where they were, lost all sense of their precarious situation. While she appreciated the distraction of his kisses, she'd also pushed aside the truth that Zach wanted to destroy her sister's happiness.

Ellen gazed at him now, the colorful Northern Lights reflecting off the snow and highlighting the masculine cut of his jaw. The man she'd gotten to know tonight didn't jibe with the heartless goal he'd professed. She realized with a sharp pang in her chest that she wanted to know more—much more— about Zach Kallen. Starting with the career that had tarnished his optimism and jaded his gentle soul.

Scooting closer to her, he tucked her under his arm and pulled her nearer his body heat. "Warm enough?"

"Mmm-hmm." She rested her head on his shoulder and turned her eyes toward the display of color in the late night sky. "You said earlier that you think about leaving your job every day. So…why haven't you?"

Beside her, his body tensed. He expelled a deep sigh that clouded in the cold air. "Where would I go?"

"Anywhere you want! It's a big world out there, Zach. You don't have to stay in Sacramento to make a difference. Heck, you don't have to stay in politics to make a difference. In fact, some would argue you have to get out of the political world to affect real change."

"Yeah, I know. God knows, I've thought about that." His tone was dark with regret. "But…what about the senator I work for? He gave me a job before I'd even graduated college. He gave me my start, gave me a great salary, helped me meet people with connections in the state—"

"Because he recognized your talent, your potential, your enthusiasm. He wanted to be sure no one else could hire you first!"

He shrugged. "Maybe. But I owe him something for all of that. How can I repay all the help he gave me by walking out on him?"

"This is the same man who is cheating on his wife and asking you to cover his tracks and keep his dirty secret? The man whose brand of politics involves clandestine deals and backroom meetings?"

Zach grunted. "Well, yeah. One of several like him in his office."

"As much as I appreciate and respect your loyalty to the senator for the help he gave you…" Ellen sat straighter and turned more fully toward Zach. His gaze lowered from the stars to meet hers. She drew a deep breath before plunging forward, a surge of emotion twisting in her chest. "This man is manipulating you, using you, playing on that sense of debt he created in you. He's dragging you down into the mud with him, and he'll kill everything that is good and honest and honorable in you if you let him." She placed her hands on his icy cheeks and drilled him with a beseeching stare. "Don't let him do that. You've paid your debt to him. Don't let his brand of politics destroy your faith and hope and happiness." Her voice cracked and moisture gathered in her eyes. "Please, Zach."

His brow furrowed, and he cleared his throat before he spoke. "Maybe. I…If I walk away from this job, it's likely I'll never get another job in Sacramento again. He has a lot of power and influence."

"He'd sabotage your career?"

"He's done it before."

Ellen scowled. "What an ass."

Zach's cheek twitched in an almost grin. "It'd be career suicide to quit my job."

"No. You'd be saving yourself. Your soul. Finding something that makes you happy. Leave California, Zach. Move to Atlanta or Albany or…or Portland."

He arched an eyebrow. "Portland isn't the capital of Oregon."

She returned a coy grin. "I know. But it's a really great place to start over. I promise to show you all around."

His nostrils flared as he sucked in a deep breath, and the Northern Lights reflected the passion that filled his eyes. He pressed a warm kiss to her lips and rested his forehead against hers. "If you ever decide to leave magazine editing and layout for a new career, you could make a mint on tour as an inspirational speaker."

"There's more to life than making money, Zach."

"So I've heard. And I'm beginning to see it for myself lately."

Hope swelled in her chest, spreading an airy warmth. "Then you'll think about quitting your job? And I mean *really* think hard about it—no guilt or second-guessing?"

His fingers combed through her hair and cradled the back of her head. "I will." He sealed the promise with a deep lingering kiss that spun a crackling energy through her.

Humming her satisfaction, Ellen angled her body so she could lean against Zach's solid strength and nestle in his embrace. Tipping her face toward the heavens, she marveled at the dancing swath of colored light on the horizon. "Beautiful." She sighed after a moment.

"Yeah. We definitely owe Santa for arranging this."

She cast Zach a curious look. "Come again?"

"If his reindeer hadn't run us off the road, I seriously doubt we'd have seen Mother Nature's awesome show. We'd have been inside asleep in our respective beds."

"Hmm. You're probably right."

"And we wouldn't have had the chance to talk the way we have. I'd have never heard about your flashing the crowd at Mardi Gras."

She groaned and covered her eyes with one hand.

A chuckle rumbled in his chest. "That is an image I'm going to savor for a very long time."

"Zach…"

He raised a hand and stroked her cheek with his thumb. "That and the way the moonlight looks when it shines on your face."

Ellen's heartbeat slowed.

"I'm glad we got this chance to know each other, Ellen. You're a special woman."

She tried to talk, to respond, but the air stuck in her throat, backed up in her lungs.

Despite the bitter cold, the uncertainty of their rescue, the inconvenience of lost sleep and hunger, Ellen couldn't think of anywhere else she'd rather be. Snuggled in Zach's arms, the night sky draped in a dazzling glow, Ellen felt something shift inside her. She knew at that moment she was right where she belonged. After giving Zach a soft kiss, she laid her head on his shoulder and closed her eyes.

"Yeah," he murmured quietly, "I definitely owe Santa's reindeer for tonight. Big-time."

Zach woke in the predawn darkness, colder than he could ever remember being in his life, despite the warm woman snuggled in his arms on the backseat. Ellen shivered violently, and he tucked her coat more securely around her and he pulled her more firmly against him.

His nose was frozen, his feet were numb, and an icy chill seeped to his bones. But morning was just a couple hours away, and the sun would raise the temperature and provide the light they needed to safely flag a passing car.

Ignoring the crick in his neck from the awkward angle at which he'd been sleeping, he tried to doze until sunrise. Sometime later, a bright shaft of sun crept over the horizon and roused him again.

Ellen was still shivering, and he did his best to chafe warmth into her arms and hands.

Pulling her scarf up around her nose, she shuddered hard as she angled her head to look at him. Despite the wrap over her half her face, tiny smile lines crinkled the corners of her eyes, and sunlight caught the sparkle of humor in her gaze.

"G-g-good m-morn-n-ning-g," she said, teeth chattering. "M-merry Christmas Eve."

"Good m—" A rumbling noise in the distance cut Zach off. He stiffened, straining his ear to listen.

"Zach, what's—?"

"Shh. Listen!" When the rumbling grew louder, more distinct, his pulse jumped. "That's a truck! Maybe even the road crew with a plow." He pushed her up and scrambled from under her to turn the ignition. He prayed the battery had enough life left that he could roll the window down one last time.

Ellen tipped her head to listen, excitement lighting her face.

With a squeak and a groan of struggle, the frozen window slid slowly down, and Zach waved Ellen forward. "Hurry! We've got to get up to the road and flag 'em down!"

Ellen scrambled out the window, and Zach followed, his cramped, cold muscles protesting. In the morning light, the slope of the embankment up to the road proved steeper than he'd believed the night before. Slicked with ice, the hill would be a challenging climb at best.

Ellen's face reflected the same dismay as she cast a worried glance at him. "Any ideas?"

"Try to gouge foot- and handholds and pull yourself up. I'll be behind you and give you a boost up to the top. But one of us has to get up there *fast,* before that truck gets out of range."

Together they started chipping at the ice-crusted snow, carving out a notch or two for her to hoist herself closer to the rim. The rumbling engine was louder now, their rescue almost upon them. But Ellen was only halfway up the hill, still six feet shy of the top, and scraping her next handhold as fast as she could.

Zach considered yelling to the driver but over the grinding of the engine and scraping blade, the chances of being heard were slim. His energy was better used digging a foothold for Ellen.

"Oh, no. There it is! Zach, I'll never make it!" Ellen tried frantically to scramble up the icy slope. Her feet slipped and skidded, and she slid all the way back to the bottom of the rise.

Zach squelched his disappointment, turned and clambered

onto the roof of the Malibu. Waving his arms, he shouted, "Hey, down here! Stop!"

A flash of color drew his attention to Ellen, who used the gouges they'd already scooped to climb halfway back up the hill. She snatched the scarf from her head, knotted it into a ball and heaved it over the rise of the hill.

A screech of hydraulic brakes echoed through the still, frozen air. She cut a glance at him, her expression a mirror of the hope that bubbled in his chest. In unison they shouted, "Help! Down here!"

A door slammed, and a red-cheeked man with a white beard peered over the top of the hill. "Land sakes, folks. You been out here all night?"

Ellen bobbed her head. "Can you take us to a phone? Please? We have to get to Spokane by two!"

"Sure enough. And you can use the radio in my truck to call a tow for your car." He disappeared for a second, then reappeared with Ellen's blue scarf in his hand. "I believe this is yours? I thought I was seeing things at first when that came sailing in from the edge of the road. Smart thinking, honey. I'd have never seen you if not for your unique distress flag there."

Ellen grinned at the elfin man, then at Zach. "Necessity is the mother of invention."

Zach scooted off the roof of the Malibu and helped Ellen down from the icy hill. Pulling her into his arms he pressed a kiss to her warm lips. "Well, sweetheart, I think we may just make it to the church on time."

She held up crossed fingers. "From your lips to God's ears!"

While Ellen maneuvered up the rope ladder the driver of the snowplow dropped for them, his thoughts turned to his original plan for today. If they made good time getting to Spokane, he might still have time to talk to Sean before the ceremony started. He still had a duty to look out for his best friend's happiness.

Even if it meant Ellen hated him.

Chapter 8

The cab of the snowplow was crowded for three people, but the blast of the heater was a welcome blessing. The driver, whose resemblance to Santa was uncanny, shared his Thermos of coffee and tin of sugar cookies with them, and Ellen devoured four cookies with gratitude, savoring the sweet treat.

Within twenty minutes, they'd reached a small town and caught the owner of a small diner just before he closed his restaurant. Borrowing a phone beside the cash register, they called Ellen's parents and assured them they were safe and en route. A second call to the car rental company secured them a replacement car and sent a tow truck out to recover the Malibu.

By 11:00 a.m., they were fed, warm and back on the re-opened interstate headed toward Spokane. But Ellen couldn't breathe easy yet. Zach's grim expression as they approached the exit for Spokane told her he hadn't abandoned his plan to interfere with the wedding. In light of the night's events and all she'd learned about Zach, his determination to talk Sean out of marrying her sister bothered Ellen all the more. She'd seen Zach's chivalry when he tended to her after the carbon-monoxide scare, his practicality in dealing with their safety and best chance for rescue, his kindness in calming her fears. How could the same man who'd showed her honor and gentleness plan to ruin his friend's wedding?

"Zach, about the wedding…you won't really…" She paused, air snagging in her chest when she locked gazes with him. With his handsome face, sense of honor and sharp intelligence, Zach could easily steal her heart. If only…

"I won't really what?"

She angled her head to watch the traffic clogging the frontage road to a large mall. "You know, I halfway hoped we wouldn't be rescued in time for the wedding. If Sean and Trix married before we got there, then you can't mess anything up for them."

His strong, warm fingers grasped her chin and brought her head around to face him. "Ellen, I told you before, my intent is not to hurt anyone or mess anything up. I hate that it's gotten so late, so close to the wedding."

She frowned and pulled her chin from his hand, even though his touch was inviting.

"Whether he gets married or not is up to Sean. I just—" He sighed and stared at the traffic in front of them. "I want a chance to lay out the truth as I see it to my friend and hear from his lips, see his face, know for sure he's considered what he's doing carefully. I have to know this is what he wants, because this is *not* what the Sean I met in college would have ever chosen of his own will. I'm trying to save him from future unhappiness. I'm sorry, Ellen, but if I think he feels at all coerced or manipulated or cornered into this marriage, I *will* try to talk him out of it."

She turned back to the view of last-minute shoppers braving the snowy roads, clogging the parking lots.

Zach sighed. "I have to do what I feel is right, even if it makes me unpopular or hated."

A bittersweet stab of regret twisted in her chest. While she admired his conviction, his determination to follow his conscience, she wished he hadn't chosen her sister's wedding as his target. Yet a whisper of doubt tickled her brain. What if Sean hadn't changed? What if Zach was right and her sister had pressured Sean into this marriage?

Ellen gritted her teeth and sent Zach a wounded look of resignation. "Fine. Do what you think you have to. But remember this—sometimes doing the right thing means listening to your heart instead of your head. Trust your heart, Zach."

Ten minutes later they pulled up in front of the church. Zach turned to Ellen, wanting to say something to smooth over the uneasiness between them, but she climbed out without speaking to him.

Shoving down his disappointment over the chasm that had opened between them, Zach stepped out of the car and stretched the kinks from his muscles. He heard the clatter of high heels on the sidewalk and spotted two women, one a sixtyish version of Ellen and the other wearing a long, dark green dress, rushing toward them.

"Oh, thank goodness! Ellen, honey, your dad and I have been so worried!" The older woman wrapped her arms around Ellen and looked as if she might not let go.

"I'm fine, Mom. Thanks to Zach." Ellen faced him, a wistfulness in her expression. "I wouldn't be here if not for him. In more ways than one."

Mrs. Davis turned to Zach on cue and treated him to the same bracing hug of welcome. "In that case, I'm forever in your debt, you darling man."

"I hate to break this up, but we've got to get a move on," the other bridesmaid said, tapping the watch on her wrist. "Ellen has forty minutes to shower, fix her hair and dress before showtime!"

Ellen's eyes widened. "Forty minutes?"

The bridesmaid tugged Ellen's arm, hauling her toward the church door, and Mrs. Davis kissed Zach's cheek.

"And you have to get in your tux, Zach. Hurry!" Ellen's mother gave him a gentle push toward a door at the other end of the building. "The groomsmen are dressing in the first room on the left through that door. Sean's waiting for you."

In a swish of perfume and taffeta, Mrs. Davis and the bridesmaid swept Ellen away. Zach shoved his hands in his pockets and hunched his shoulders against the stiff icy breeze as he watched her leave. She gave him one last look over her shoulder before she disappeared into the church, hustled along by her escorts.

A cold emptiness settled in Zach's chest in her absence. Until she was gone, Zach hadn't realized how much he'd depended on her to buoy his spirits through the treacherous trip from Seattle and the long frigid night in the wintry elements.

She'd given him credit for getting her to Spokane, to the church, but he hadn't done it alone. They'd survived the harrowing experience together, the experience far less dreary because they'd had each other to rely on, to keep each other's morale up. The two stronger as a team than alone.

A tingle rippled down his spine. A team...

"Zach!"

Sean's shout lifted Zach out of his reverie, before the conclusion nipping his heels could fully form. Giving Sean a wave, Zach grabbed his backpack from the backseat and headed into the church.

He'd no sooner stepped inside the welcoming warmth of the church than Sean slapped a garment bag in his hand. "Your tux. Shake a leg, pal. Service starts soon." Then pumping his hand, Sean added, "You gave us a scare, dude. After the wedding, I want to hear all about the accident and your night with Trixie's sister."

Zach steeled himself. No time like the present. With the ceremony minutes away, he might not get another chance to have his talk with Sean. "Actually, I need to speak to you...now. Before the service starts."

Sean frowned as he hustled Zach into the makeshift dressing room for the groomsmen. "Can you talk and dress at the same time?"

"I— Yeah. Whatever." Zach slipped off his shoes and gathered his thoughts. "Sean, are you sure you want to marry Trixie? Can you honestly tell me you're marrying her because you want to and not because you have to?"

Sean paused in the middle of pulling Zach's suit out of the garment bag. He blinked, stunned. "Is this a joke?"

"No joke." He unfastened the buttons on his shirt then paused, facing his former roommate. "I have to ask, because… well, I remember what you were like in college. Back then, you scorned the idea of marriage before you were forty. You would never have committed yourself to one woman."

Sean laughed. "You're right."

"So…what changed?"

"Well…"

While he waited for Sean to form his answer, Zach noticed they had company. He did a double take. "Uh, Sean…is that a cat?"

Sean glanced to the chair where a large tabby sat blinking at them…wearing a bow tie. "Yeah. That's Trixie's cat, Buttons. He's the ring bearer."

Zach snorted a laugh. "Excuse me? You have a cat in your wedding party?"

Sean rolled his eyes and grinned sheepishly. "Trixie's idea. Neither of us have a young nephew to do the job, and she considers her cat family, so—" He shrugged. "Whatever Trixie wants."

Zach frowned then waved a hand at the cat. "See, this is what I mean. *You* would never have a cat in the wedding if it were up to you. But you're doing stuff out of character for you, because Trixie wants it. What about what *you* want?"

Sean gave him a withering glance. "It's no big deal. Get dressed, will you?"

"Sean, I don't want you to wake up in ten years and find you made a mistake. Is this wedding—is Trixie what you want? It's not too late to back out."

Squaring his shoulders, Sean stepped closer to Zach and met his best man's eyes. "This is what I want. When I said all that stuff in college, I didn't know how one woman could change your life, change your view of things, make you want different things for yourself and your future. I love Trix. She fills up a place inside me that was empty before. She gives me a happiness I never knew possible. Ten years from now I will still want Trixie, I will still love Trixie, and I will still be happy, because she is everything to me. She is the only woman I want."

The sincerity and intensity in Sean's expression startled Zach. Took the steam out of his argument. Zach released a slow breath, feeling the tension that had him wound tight release its grip.

"Someday you'll meet someone who'll turn your world upside down, and you'll understand," Sean added, and Zach's heart performed a slow roll in his chest.

"Now, if that's all, I'll let you dress. Be ready in ten minutes, okay?" Sean paused at the door and aimed a finger at the cat. "Oh, yeah. As my best man, you're in charge of Buttons."

Zach placed the fur-ball ring bearer on the podium next to Sean and dusted cat hair from the tux as he took his place at the altar. The groom gave him a crooked smile.

He had resigned himself to Sean's decision, although a few doubts still niggled inside him, when the organist began playing the processional. Clasping his hands behind his back, Zach glanced to the back of the church to watch the bridesmaids enter the sanctuary.

And caught his breath.

Ellen was at the back of the line of women, gliding gracefully to the altar rail, and in the past forty minutes, she'd been transformed. Pinned up with soft tendrils framing her face, her hair shone with golden highlights. The beautiful face he'd admired in the moonlight last night had been emphasized with just the right application of makeup, and the emerald-green dress she wore brought out the sparkle in her green eyes and defined the womanly curves her bulky coat had hidden. Sprigs of baby's breath in her hair reminded him of the sprinkling of snowflakes that had shimmered on her eyelashes and shoulders last night. His winter fairy looked every bit as beautiful and elegant as a Christmas princess.

Someday you'll meet someone who'll turn your world upside down, and you'll understand.

"I already have," he murmured to himself.

His acknowledgment of what Ellen had come to mean to him rattled Zach to the marrow. He frowned, realizing how much he wanted Ellen to be a part of his future, realizing Ellen might not return his feelings, realizing the geographic and emotional distance they still had between them.

Her anxious gaze sought his, and when their eyes met, his chest filled with a warmth and joy that expanded until he couldn't breathe. He'd never felt a rush of emotion so pure and sweet in his life and knew something significant was happening in that moment. His life was about to change.

He also knew he was responsible for the nervous look she wore. His serious expression had to have added to her uncertainty over his intentions. Zach longed to hold her, soothe her, assure her he'd come to grips with Sean's decision. The best he could do for the moment, however, was send her a smile. Her brow knit, as if she were trying to decipher his silent message, and she bit her bottom lip.

Heat flashed through him at the prospect of nibbling that plump lip himself in the days to come.

When Ellen tore her gaze away, sending an equally worried glance toward Sean, Zach glanced to the groom himself. And jolted at the expression that lit his college friend's face.

Sean's smile couldn't have been broader, his smile brighter, his eyes damper. The love and confidence that glowed in Sean's eyes were as pure and genuine as Zach had ever seen. Turning slightly, Zach followed the direction of Sean's gaze to find Trixie walking slowly down the aisle with an identical joy and affection warming her face.

Zach's heart thumped. The naked emotion and happiness in

his best friend's eyes was a mirror of the warmth that had filled Zach's chest when he'd seen Ellen walking toward the altar.

And suddenly it clicked. He got it.

He understood the love that had changed his womanizing roommate into a devoted groom. He knew the happiness and desire that made Sean want to spend his life with Trixie. Because he knew he could share the same love and longing for a future with Ellen. His head spun with the possibilities and the challenges his realization wrought. He weighed the sacrifices he'd gladly make for Ellen.

"If there is anyone here who knows why these two should not lawfully be wed, let them speak now or forever hold their peace," the minister intoned, bringing Zach's attention to the ceremony in progress.

Sean sent him a warning glare. Trixie divided a curious glance between Zach and her groom.

And Ellen lifted an anxious stare to meet Zach's gaze.

Zach shrugged and grinned. "Not me. I'm good."

Sean chuckled and drew his bride closer.

Ellen released an audible sigh of relief, her lips curling in a grateful smile. Zach continued to exchange stolen glances and secret smiles with Ellen until the bride and groom led the recession out of the sanctuary. After gathering the docile, feline ring bearer, whom Zach was convinced had been sedated for the ceremony, he met Ellen at the head of the aisle and offered his arm. Together they fell in step behind the newlyweds to exit the church.

"Thank you for not saying anything," she whispered to him.

"Actually, I did."

When Ellen raised a startled look, he chuckled and kissed her forehead. "But Sean convinced me he was making the right choice. Who am I to stand in the way of true love?"

Her eyes warmed, and her mouth tugged into a grin.

As they stepped into the narthex, Trixie rushed over to get her cat. Zach turned the pliant ring bearer over to his mistress and grabbed Ellen's hand as she started to step away.

"Hey, I was wondering…"

Her expectant gaze lifted.

"Am I still welcome at your house for Christmas?"

She squeezed his fingers. "Of course."

"Then I'd like to come. We can talk about new possibilities for employment, other ways I can change the world besides politics."

Ellen blinked and furrowed her brow. "What?"

"You were right about my needing to leave the job that was sucking my soul. I'm going to turn in my two-weeks' notice in January."

Her face brightened. "That's great, Zach. You deserve to be happy."

"I'm glad you think so, because…you're a big part of what makes me happy. The biggest part."

The smile on her lips slipped. "Zach?"

"I want to come to Portland. I want to spend more time with you and see what develops."

Her mouth opened and shut soundlessly, her shock written in her wide eyes.

Zach's gut tightened. Had he presumed too much? Nothing said Ellen returned his feelings. He drew a deep restorative breath and plunged on, risking it all for the promise of love and happiness he'd found, stranded with his bridesmaid on a snowy winter night.

"I'm falling in love with you, Ellen. Last night I found everything that was missing in my life…with you." He swallowed the knot of trepidation climbing his throat. "I want you to be a part of my future. You make me happy."

She hesitated, searching his face as if verifying his honesty. "Was there a question in there somewhere? Something about how I feel and what I want?"

His pulse kicked. "I—well…how *do* you feel? What *do* you want?"

Her cheek dimpled as she flashed a lopsided grin and wrapped her arms around his neck. "I feel lucky to have met you, Zach Kallen, and I don't want anything."

Zach's heart sank. "You don't? Nothing?"

"Nope." She leaned into him, and he saw the spark of amusement in her evergreen eyes. "Last night, Santa gave me everything I'd been hoping for, too." She brushed a kissed across his lips and sighed happily. "You are the best Christmas present I could ask for."

Dipping his head, he captured her lips and poured his heart into a deep, soul-shaking kiss. As the church bells began to ring, celebrating the newlyweds' union, Zach's spirits soared. "Merry Christmas, sweetheart."

* * * * *

SANTA UNDER COVER

Sharron McClellan

To the Cowan Family (Barb, Jim, Mickey and Alissa,
Corey, Brett, Mo, the Boys and everybody else)—
thank you for all the wonderful Christmas memories.
It still doesn't seem like the Holidays
unless I have "Tom and Jerry" mix in the fridge…

Love you,
Sharron

Chapter 1

"No, you can't have chocolate." Gwyneth Colton glanced at one of the three children following her through the Bellevue Mall, little hand clutching little hand so they formed a human chain with her as the anchor. "I'm not sending you back with a sugar buzz. Your moms would have a fit."

She steeled herself, waiting for the whining and begging that was sure to follow.

"Okay," six-year-old Connor replied. No complaining. No tantrum. Certainly no whining or begging. Just quiet acceptance that he wasn't getting what he wanted. Again.

Or ever.

Why couldn't they be spoiled brats? She had little experience with children, but since they'd arrived at the mall to visit Santa, she'd seen enough of *those* children to know what to expect. They demanded. Screamed. Called their parents names and said they hated them.

But living in a women's shelter, these kids were anything

but spoiled, and Connor's simple reply told her just how much her expectations were off.

And that the attitude problem wasn't theirs. It was hers.

Gwyn sighed, wishing she could blame work. When she'd become a private investigator, she'd thought it would be exciting. Instead, her days were spent photographing people who wanted to defraud insurance companies or taking pictures of philandering spouses.

All in all, it left her bored and a bit depressed.

And she couldn't blame Richard, either. Her latest boyfriend, he'd broken up with her just before the holiday season. But she'd always known he wasn't forever. He was something to do on the weekend.

No, neither crappy relationship nor boring job could account for her bad attitude. The fault was hers and hers alone. She was angry at herself for settling. Settling for a boyfriend that didn't love her. Settling for cases that left her empty.

Gwyn bent down, her thick, waist-length blond hair falling forward, until she was level with Connor and the other two children. "Tell you what. After we visit Santa, we'll buy some candy." Their eyes widened. She smiled, warmed by their reaction. "Frangos for everyone?"

The "Godiva of the Pacific Northwest" chocolates might be a little rich for the kids—heck, they'd be happy with a Hershey bar—but it was Christmas, and Frangos was a Seattle tradition.

They grinned at her in unison, and the two boys erupted with small cheers as their answer. Then quiet, dark-haired, five-year-old Allie leaned in. "Thank you," she whispered.

So polite. Such good kids. Gwyn blinked back sudden, surprising tears. "Okay, let's go see Santa."

Rising onto her toes, she scanned the area until she spotted Santa's Snowman Village, a long line of children—and her sister, Glory. Standing near the front of the line and dressed in a gold-threaded sweater that was the match to her own, her sister was hard to miss.

Glory spotted her, as well, and waved her over.

"Okay, everyone, Santa is up ahead." All three pulled on her arm at the announcement, eager to get in line. Michael broke free of the pack.

"Wait. Wait!" she shouted. A flicker of panic washing over her, Gwyn raised her voice just enough to let them know she meant it while she clutched the boy's jacket, yanking him to a stop. She breathed a quiet sigh of relief. If he'd gotten away... If she'd lost him...

"I need you all to stay with me," she said, willing her heart to stop pounding.

"Or we get on the naughty list?" Connor asked.

"Maybe," Gwyn said, trying not to smile at his solemn expression. "Let's just make sure that doesn't happen."

She hurried the kids toward Glory. "Isn't this great?" her sister said, hugging Gwyn as the kids fell into line with Glory's two kids from the shelter.

Great? Outside, the rain had turned to ice and was growing worse, parking had been a nightmare, and the thickness of the crowds tested her nerves in a way she never thought possible.

Despite the negatives, Gwyn couldn't be irritated. Not when Glory beamed at her and the kids chattered and laughed as they waited.

"Except for the lack of eggnog with rum, yes," Gwyn said.

"Well, I can't offer you nog, but I can offer you eye candy," Glory teased. Winding her arm through Gwyn's, she nodded toward one of the elves milling about near Santa. "What do you think of him?"

Gwyn resisted the urge to roll her eyes at her sister's blatant tactics to fix her up and reminded herself that Glory was just trying to help.

But there would be no dating. Not right now. In the spirit of being "Richard-free" and tired of being the bearer of bad news that broke up another marriage, she'd promised herself she'd remain single until she figured out what she wanted. For Christmas, she'd focus on the things that mattered. Like family, and fidelity and being true to herself.

"A bit tall for an elf, isn't he?" Gwyn said, trying not to stare. Whoever he was, he needed to lay off the candy canes. His thick, green tights left nothing to the imagination.

"Not him," Glory said. "Santa."

"You think Santa is hot? That's wrong," Gwyn whispered, even as she turned her attention to the man in red. Watching him through her lashes, she saw him lift a child off his lap, the motion causing his beard to swing outward.

It wasn't much, but from her angle it was enough to reveal a man not much older than her and with a strong jaw shaded by a day's worth of dark growth. Couple that with broad shoulders that pulled at his padded costume and Gwyn began to reconsider her "no dating" vow.

Hot Santa. "Really wrong," she finished, still staring.

"Yeah, you sound appalled," Glory said, laughing. "You should let him know what you'd like for Christmas. I bet he has *something* you'd want."

No doubt. Gwyn kept the thought to herself. There was no point in encouraging her sister. "You need help."

"And you need a decent boyfriend with a big—"

"Glory!"

"—heart," Glory finished.

"*Professional* help," Gwyn said.

The elf waved Connor forward, and the tow-headed child looked up at Gwyn. "Go on," she said, and before she finished the short sentence, Connor bolted up the two short stairs. In seconds, he was on Santa's lap, whispering what he wanted.

Gwyn smiled at the scene. This was why she'd come.

Less than a minute later, and with the gratuitous candy cane in hand, the boy hugged Santa and jumped down. Gwyn waved at Connor. "Wait over there," she called out, pointing at an oversize gingerbread man on the far side of the fake candy bridge. Grinning, Connor plopped down at the cookie's feet, eyeing his candy cane but not opening it.

"You're next," she said to Allie, giving her a nudge.

Instead of running up the stairs, the little girl clutched Gwyn's leg, burying her face against her denim-clad thigh.

"I think you'll have to go with her," Glory said. "Maybe you can sit on Santa's lap." Snickers raced through the crowd behind them from both kids and parents.

Gwyn's cheeks heated. "Please, speak up," she said over her shoulder. "I don't think the North Pole heard you."

Glory grinned then stuck her tongue out.

Resisting the urge to flip her sister off, Gwyn smoothed Allie's hair. "It's okay. You don't have to go."

The little girl's eyes welled with tears.

Oh, crap. Gwyn's heart beat harder. What was wrong now? She told her she didn't have to go. "You want to go?" Gwyn asked, taking a shot as to the reason behind the unexpected waterworks.

Allie held up her arms in the international sign for "pick me up."

"Santa's lap," Glory whispered in her ear.

"Bite me," Gwyn whispered back. Looking at Santa, she shrugged, at a loss as to what to do. Was she even allowed to go up there? He crooked his finger, motioning her to come forward, his eyes smiling as he answered her silent question.

Great. Glory was going to love this. With a determined sigh, Gwyn picked up Allie. "Come on, sweetie." The little girl wrapped around her arms round her neck as Gwyn climbed the steps.

"Hi, Santa." Gwyn said, trying not to stare into his eyes. Vivid, bright green eyes. Like holly. And while the skin around them was unmarred by wrinkles, there was something in his gaze that told her this Santa had seen more to life than most.

Then he smiled at her—a broad grin behind a white beard that made her knees weak.

Hot Santa.

The litany tripped through her head, and she reminded herself that she was not here to ogle the man in red. She blinked. "This is Allie."

"Hi, Allie." His deep voice was as warm and reassuring as a down blanket. "Do you want to talk to me?"

Other than a brief nod, Allie remained motionless.

This time, Santa glanced past them. "There are other kids waiting, Allie. And I have to leave soon to get to the North Pole and help pack the sleigh."

The beard might hide his facial expression, but his point wasn't lost on Gwyn.

Allie whimpered, the sound almost imperceptible it was so quiet. There was only one solution. Taking a deep breath, she moved closer. With Allie still in her arms, Gwyn sat on Santa's lap, ignoring the laughs behind her.

He "oofed" under their weight. Despite that, his thighs felt firm beneath her. He placed his hand on the small of her back, fingers splayed, and sending shivers up her spine.

Hot Santa? Oh, God, yes.

She swallowed, trying to ignore the shivers as they rippled outward. "Allie, can you tell Santa what you want for Christmas?" she asked, hoping she seemed more nonchalant than she felt.

"Barbie," was the whispered answer.

"A Barbie it is," Santa said, chuckling. His green eyes met Gwyn's. "How about you? What can I bring you for Christmas?"

A series of replies flickered through her head, and all guaranteed to put her on the naughty list that Connor talked about. Swallowing hard, she smiled at him, ignoring the urge to yank down the white cotton and see the more of the man behind the beard. "Pencil me in for a Barbie, too."

"You're not too old?"

"Old?" Her mouth dropped open in mock outrage. "I am not—"

The lights in the mall died, leaving them in darkness and cutting her off as the Snowman Village erupted in screams. Allie's grip on Gwyn's neck tightened into a stranglehold, and Gwyn clutched Santa's shoulder, steadying herself.

"It's okay," she said, trying to soothe the little girl. "It's just the storm. The lights will be on in a minute."

The lights flickered back to life with her words. Relieved, Gwyn looked at the line. Glory had the kids in a group around her. Their eyes met. *Thanks,* she mouthed.

Still sitting on Santa's lap, she turned to check on Connor. He stood next to the oversize cookie, his eyes wide with fear, clutching the candy cane as if it were a life preserver.

Her stomach tightened. Oh, no. This wasn't good. She started to rise. "Connor, stay—"

Once again, the lights flickered and died. Around them, the shouts of panic increased, and Santa jerked her back down to his lap. "Stay put," he said. "It's safer than stumbling around in the dark."

He had a point. Especially considering she had a small child stuck to her like a limpet. "Okay."

"What's your name?" Santa's voice filtered through the shouts.

Gwyn's head snapped toward him. "Excuse me?" Was he hitting on her? Now? He might be hot, but no one was that hot.

"I'm not trying to pick you up," he said. She didn't need to see him to hear his exasperation. "If the lights don't come back on in a minute, we might have a *situation.* So a name would be useful."

A situation? The emphasis sounded ominous and specific and made her wonder what Hot Santa did when he wasn't playing the jolly old elf.

"Gwyn," she replied.

"I'm Nick."

She continued, "Thrilled to meet you. Now, if you could just hold Allie for a second, I have a scared little boy—"

"He'll be fine," Nick said, cutting her off.

Gwyn knew better. She'd seen Connor's face. Eyes wide. Feet itching to run away from whatever it was that scared him.

The dark perhaps? Being alone in the dark?

The emergency lights came on, casting their red-tinted beams over the crowds, and Gwyn jumped to her feet, anxious to get to Connor and sure that he'd be a crying mess of kid by now.

It was worse.

The little boy was gone.

Chapter 2

Even as chaos erupted around him, Detective Nick Linton willed his heartbeat to slow and his muscles to remain loose. He'd spent all day sitting at the Bellevue Mall, waiting for the Christmas Bandits to strike. Now was not the time to lose it.

The Christmas Bandits…a cheerily, ironic name for a group of murderous thieves. But clever, he reminded himself. Tricky as hell, they had followed the same modus operandi for the past several years. They'd hit a well-known mall jewelry store on Christmas Eve, leave without detection and then disappear.

When they popped back onto the radar, it would be in the Pacific Northwest but in a different city, a different state and a different chain of stores that specialized in diamonds.

No one had connected the dots and figured out the different hits were made by the same people until last year when they left behind the store clerk and the cop that tried to save him. Both dead.

It was disturbing enough when a civilian was killed, but when one of their own was murdered it became personal. Soon the investigation uncovered the truth. Now, thanks to a chatty informant, here he was. Not that it mattered now.

Not when a child was missing.

Tuning out both Gwyn and the panicked shouts from the shoppers, Nick scrutinized the scene. Cops dressed as elves worked the crowd to control the stampede toward the exits. Good. Peering past the chaos and into the shadows, he searched for signs of abduction. Nothing suspicious came into view. No child being dragged against his will. No blond-haired boy lying limp in someone's arms. Nothing.

He stretched his fingers, releasing some of the mounting tension and grabbed the police-issue walkie-talkie from behind the Santa chair. "We have a possible abduction. I want all exits shut except the south one. Over."

"You got it. Out."

"Where's Connor?" The woman waiting in line with Gwyn—Nick guessed a sibling since they looked and dressed too much alike to be anything else—hurried up the stairs, trailed by three children.

"I don't know," Gwyn replied, as calm and controlled as if nothing had happened.

Impressive. Most women would be hysterical by now.

She continued, "Santa here is working with the police to find him."

And despite her own desperate shouting she noticed details, such as his orders and the fact he was a cop. Not many people were that level-headed in a crisis.

"What do you mean, you don't know?" the woman asked, her voice shooting up an octave.

Not as calm as her sister. Too bad. It would make this easier, but it wasn't the first time he'd worked with a person on the edge of panic.

Nick placed a firm hand on the woman's shoulder. "What's your name?"

"Glory." Her jaw trembled, and while a twinge of sympathy moved him, there wasn't time for pity or niceties.

"Glory, we're heading toward the south exit," Nick said, motioning her to move. "Watch for any sign of Connor as we walk. If someone took him, he might have a hat on. A different jacket. Anything to disguise him. I have men waiting at the doors. We don't want anyone to slip by without going past you."

For a moment, the group stared at him, the children's mouths hanging open. There was no doubt they'd never see Santa the same way again, but it couldn't be helped.

"You heard Santa," Gwyn said, her voice remained level but carried an urgent undertone that snapped the group to attention. She turned her blue-eyed stare toward Nick. "This will go faster if you help carry a kid or two." She handed Allie to her sister.

"And what do you think you're doing?" Nick asked, following the movement.

She leaned in toward him, pushing aside the cotton beard just enough to whisper, "I don't want to get Glory's hopes up, but I don't think he was abducted." Her breath was warm against his ear. "If you'd seen Connor's face...the panic. I think he ran and hid. I'll stay to search for him while you take Glory to the south entrance."

She spoke as if they were partners, and Nick bit back a retort and focused on her words. Hiding? Possible. He wouldn't discount the option, but leaving a layperson behind to do the job of a cop was *not* an option. There were too many uncontrolled variables in her suggestion. What if she was wrong and stumbled on the abductor? Or even the Bandits? Of course, it was more likely they'd abandon any robbery plans under the surprising circumstances, but he wasn't willing to risk anyone's safety on that bet.

He shook his head. "You go with us."

She grabbed his bicep. "You're not listening, and I'm not going. I'm staying here. Connor was my responsibility, and I am not leaving until I find him."

Ah, guilt and honor—the true crux of the problem—and

much like sympathy, emotions he couldn't indulge in either himself or someone else. He peeled her fingers away. "This is not a request."

Even in the dim lighting, fury flashed in her eyes as she glared at him. For a moment, he thought she might argue. He tensed, ready to call for backup and have her hauled away if needed.

Then behind the pale blue depths, the fury shifted. "Of course."

She didn't break his gaze. Didn't fidget. She even sounded agreeable. Almost contrite. And totally truthful. He didn't believe any of it. He may have only known her a few minutes, but it was enough to know that she wasn't the kind of person who gave in that easily, which meant she was a great liar with good intentions.

A cop's worst nightmare.

Liar or not, he didn't have time to argue or question. Seconds wasted could mean the difference between finding Connor today or seeing his name on the front of a billboard for the next ten years.

Taking a kid in each arm, he nodded toward the south entrance. "Stay close."

They reached the south entrance, and Gwyn whistled in appreciation. Cops manned the doors, allowing singles and couples to leave on the left and middle, while people with children waited on the right. Luckily, the line wasn't even twenty families deep as of yet.

Nick and his men had done well, but that didn't surprise her. He was a take-charge man, and it made sense that his men were the same. But why were they staking out the mall on Christmas Eve? And it was a stakeout, she was sure of that much.

"I want one of you on each side," Nick said. She glanced at him, curiosity about his mission overwhelmed by the more urgent need to ditch the policeman and return to the Snowman Village. Still in his Santa suit, he handed off his two kids to the boys in blue and motioned for her and Glory to do the same.

She handed Michael to a uniformed man, giving him a squeeze first. "It'll be okay."

"What about the kids?" Glory asked, setting Allie down. "They can't just stand here."

The young officer raised his hand in response then kneeled down. "Who wants to see a real police car? I'll even run the siren."

Small cheers erupted in response. Gwyn's throat tightened, remembering how they'd done the same when she said she'd get the chocolate. How Connor had cheered. And then the fear that overwhelmed him when the lights went out.

"Move it." Nick placed his hand on the small of Gwyn's back, directing her to the door as the children left while Glory hurried to take position and watch for Connor.

She hesitated. Perhaps Nick was right. Perhaps Connor was kidnapped. But her gut insisted otherwise, drowning out everything else and leaving her no choice.

She had to get back to the scene. Now.

Not that she planned to tell Nick. Been there, tried that. "I need to use the ladies' room first," Gwyn said. "I've been holding it since I got to the mall."

"Now is not the time," Nick said. Even the white, cotton beard couldn't hide his anger.

Gwyn swallowed the urge to tell him the truth.

"Just hurry," Glory broke in.

Good enough. Let Nick keep his disappointment. If she found Connor, it wouldn't matter. Turning on her heel, she rushed down the wide hallway, past the departing shoppers and past the ladies' room.

Breaking into a jog, she headed back toward the Snowman Village. If Connor were anywhere, it was in that area. Perhaps in a corner. Maybe under the yards of cotton fluff that served as snow and resembled a blanket that would offer a hiding spot. Wherever he was, she'd find him.

As long as she did it before Nick figured out she was gone. Still jogging, she glanced backward. People flowed toward the south exit, and there was no sign of Nick.

Hot Santa.

She kicked the phrase from her mind. It figured that he was

a cop. Not that she disliked cops. She respected them more than most. She knew how hard they worked, and the fact they got anything done under the legal constraints that hemmed them in was amazing.

But right now, they were the enemy. Or Nick was.

Ahead of her, Santa's chair glittered in the dim, red-tinted lights.

I'm coming, Connor. Her heart slammed hard against the walls of her chest as she ran faster.

She stopped at the edge of the Snowman Village. "Be here," she whispered, leaning over, hands on her thighs to catch her breath. "Please be here." Standing, she cupped her hands around her mouth. "Connor!"

"This isn't the ladies' room."

Nick. Gwyn exhaled with a sigh. "And you're not Connor."

"You're supposed to be watching the doors."

Thank you, Captain Obvious. "I got lost."

Hands on her hips, she faced her opponent. He still wore the Santa pants held up by suspenders but gone was the red hat, the beard, the coat and the grin. Replacing them were a black T-shirt, a deep frown and confirmation that he was as hot as she imagined.

No, hotter.

"Is that the story you want to go with?" he asked, with no visible sense of humor.

Hot cop. The thought popped into her head, forcing its way past the panic and the fear and the dread. Goose bumps swept up her arms. "I didn't see you following me."

"You weren't supposed to."

She crossed her arms over her chest, rubbing the goose bumps away. Hot or not, skilled or not, she wasn't going back. Not without Connor.

Nick stepped closer, breaking her invisible personal space barrier. She held her ground. "Short of carrying me out of here, I'm not leaving," Gwyn said.

Nick didn't say a word.

And the urge to break the silence and say something, anything, overwhelmed her. "Ten minutes," she blurted. "Give me that."

Still, he offered nothing. No words to show she'd swayed him in either direction.

A wave of frustration washed through Gwyn. They covered a number of situations in P.I. training—computer searches, basic law and she'd taken a *Krav Maga* course so she could fight off an assailant if necessary.

But they'd never covered facing down a cop in a missing-child situation.

Taking a deep breath, she knew what she had to do. The only thing she could do that might break through his tough, law-abiding cop exterior.

Her eyes locked with his, she placed a hand on his chest, willing him to feel her fear, and her almost-painful need to set things right. "Please," she begged. "Please help me."

Chapter 3

Gwyn held her breath, watching as Nick ran a hand through his hair making the short, black strands stick up.

He shook his head.

Her eyes flooded with angry tears, but she blinked them away, refusing to give him the satisfaction of seeing her cry. Not that *he* cared, but *she* sure as hell did.

"I am going to catch more crap for this…" He shook his head again. "Don't make me regret saying yes."

She realized that he wasn't denying her help. He was chastising himself for agreeing to assist her. She took a step back in surprise at the unexpected answer. "I won't let you down." She smiled up at him. "Thank you."

"Don't thank me yet," Nick said, anger giving him an edge that made her want to back away even farther. "You get ten minutes. If we don't find him by then, we go back to the south entrance. Agreed?"

Gwyn sensed that if she didn't agree, there would be no

search, and he'd take her back to Glory, willing or not. "Agreed," she replied, not caring about the fury that roiled beneath his skin. Let him rant. Let him fume. She had ten minutes to locate Connor before the little kid had a nervous breakdown, and that was where her focus would remain.

"We start here," Nick said, gesturing at the Snowman Village.

"Shouldn't we split up?" Gwyn asked, peering into the shadows that surrounded them. Between the kiosks that lined the wide walkways and the Village, there were a lot of places for a small child to hide and little time to search. "We'll cover a lot more ground that way."

Despite the dim, emergency lighting, Gwyn didn't miss the unexpected expression of alarm that flickered across Nick's strong features, obliterating the irritation that seemed to be a pervasive part of his personality. "We stick together."

"Not a problem," she said, not wanting to push his grudging goodwill too far.

Slowly, they walked through Snowman Village, Gwyn calling Connor's name as they lifted up yards of cotton snow, hoping with each yard to find Connor and fighting disappointment when he wasn't there.

A long shot, she knew, but an option that couldn't be ignored.

"I take it you're the aunt," Nick said as they worked their way to the back half of the Village with still no sign of Connor.

"What?" Gwyn glanced at him, surprised at the sudden comment.

"The aunt. Connor is Glory's kid, isn't he?"

He was wrong on both counts, but it was still an interesting observation. Was her lack of maternal instincts that obvious or was it something else? She rolled up a large piece of fleecy cotton and set it aside. "Why would you think I'm the aunt?"

"She panicked. You didn't."

Made sense but it still didn't make him right. Nice to know that super cop made a few errors, even if they were minor ones. "Actually, he doesn't belong to either of us," Gwyn said glancing to watch his reaction to a scenario that hadn't passed through his logical, cop brain.

"Oh?" He dropped a large piece of fluff, his expression one of interest but nothing more.

So much for trying to tweak a cop.

"He's a kid from the shelter. Glory's a social worker," she said. "We were taking the kids out for the day. Something fun to get their minds off of their crappy accommodations."

Admiration flickered through his green-eyed gaze, and he gave her a slow nod of support. "Very Christmassy."

An odd, almost silly phrase from a decidedly non-silly man, but there was no sarcasm in his tone. No quiet malice.

He meant it.

Unexpected warmth flooded Gwyn at the praise, working its way to her toes, the tips of her fingers and touched her cheeks, leaving her flushed and more vulnerable than she cared to feel. She ducked her head and lifted back the last piece of cotton to reveal nothing but empty space.

"Perhaps," Gwyn said, making a slow circle as the chill of failure replaced the warmth of Nick's praise. "But this was not what we planned."

"No one ever plans on losing a kid," Nick said. He took her hand in his, and with a surprising tenderness, he guided her toward the south entrance. "It's not your fault."

Gwyn didn't miss the gesture. He might sympathize, but he wanted to leave and thought he could get her to go without a fight.

She wasn't that gullible, and she didn't give up that easily. Couldn't give up when she thought of Connor lost in the dark. She yanked her hand from his. "We should search the kiosks."

The corners of his mouth turned downward, and she knew what he thought because it was the same thought that ran through her head—*long shot.*

Too long.

"The kiosks were still open when the lights went out," he

said, confirming her assumption. "If he went into one, he'd have been found."

"Maybe he snuck into one afterward." Yes, the argument was weak, but anything was better than the alternative—that Nick was right, and a stranger had Connor.

Nick pushed a strand of hair away from her cheek, his eyes deep with sympathy. "I know you want to believe he's here, but we're wasting time."

"Maybe he snuck in one when he saw us leave." His touch left her lightheaded, and she wished the proffered tenderness wasn't based on sympathy and logic. "Connor wouldn't know we'd come back."

"You've been calling his name. He hasn't responded."

"You said you'd give me ten minutes," Gwyn interrupted. Nick's hand fell to his side.

Gwyn swallowed hard, determined to finish what she'd started. "I have two minutes left if you count the fact we've been standing here talking when we should be searching."

She headed to the right. "I'll take this side. You take the other."

"We need to stick together."

"Two minutes." She paused, beating back the vulnerability and fear. "Don't make me beg. Not again."

Slowly, he turned her around to face him. His eyes darted across her face and drank her in, making her feel more naked than if she were stripped down to her red satin panties.

A few seconds later, he nodded. "Two minutes," he said, and headed in the opposite direction.

She wasn't sure what he'd seen, her desperation perhaps, but she was glad it worked. Hurrying over to the closest kiosk, she stuck her head under the heavy plastic and shone her flashlight inside. Cheap sunglasses lined the wire racks. More expensive brands were locked in glass cases. But no Connor.

Four more kiosks later and her frustration was reaching an almost unbearable level.

"Where are you, kiddo," she muttered, rubbing her eyes. "Why don't you answer?"

As much as she hated to admit it, searching the kiosks had been the wrong way to go. She knew it. Nick knew it. The plastic kiosk covers were heavier than they appeared. If Connor had run into one of the booths, it would have been before they closed.

Which meant he was in one of the shops.

Or abducted.

She pushed aside the horror that the word produced and glanced at her watch. Thirty seconds left. Maybe.

Walking fast, she headed to the perimeter and past the shops, shining her flashlight through the metal gratings, watching for movement and listening for a sigh or crying—any sign that might indicate Connor was there.

The stores were as silent as the rest of the mall. Then a glimmer caught her eye. She read the sign over the frontage, *Elite Jewelry*.

She flicked off her flashlight.

A white glow shone from beneath a crack in the door. It was faint, a flashlight like hers, but it was a light. It flickered again, as if someone walked in front of it then away.

Then she heard something. Like a kitten crying.

Or a child. The heavy door muffled it, but she knew the sound of tears and terror.

Connor.

Her pulse skipped into overdrive, her world narrowed to a fine point until there was nothing and no one left but her, Connor and the fact she had to get to him. "Nick, I found him," she called out.

She grabbed the metal gate, determined to break the lock with sheer strength if needed, but it shot upward, unlocked.

"Gwyn, wait!" Nick called out, but she was already moving past glass cases full of engagement rings, necklaces and bracelets made for the über-wealthy of the east side.

"Connor!" she called his name again as she pushed open the door, flashlight raised and ready to take him into her arms.

Two steps into the room, she froze. "Oh, hell."

A tall man dressed in black waited on the other side. One gloved hand covered Connor's mouth. The other held a Sig Sauer 9mm, the open end pointed at her.

And she knew why Nick and his men were at the mall.

Chapter 4

Nick watched from the shadow of the door as one of the Christmas Bandits pointed a gun at Gwyn, using Connor as cover. Well, as much cover as a six-year-old boy could provide for a man that cleared six feet.

His hands clenched into tight fists at seeing them in danger, and the primal urge to tackle the gunman and beat him senseless almost overwhelmed reason. Almost. Instead, reason won out, and he unclenched his grip and assessed the scene, remaining as detached as possible, knowing it was the best way to help them.

So far, only one gunman was in view. Dark hair. Goatee. No visible scars. But the sound of drilling told him that the man wasn't alone, which meant that he couldn't pull his weapon without putting Gwyn and Connor at risk.

A flash of the gunman's last victims flashed through Nick's mind—bodies on the marble floor with their heads splattered all over the shiny glass cases that had once held diamonds.

He'd be damned if he was going to let that happen. He had to protect Gwyn. Protect Connor. This meant he had to join them, despite what the "Handbook" said about not being taken hostage.

Shaking his head and sure that if he lived he'd be demoted, Nick stepped into the doorway. The gunman's eyes widened then narrowed. "You." He waved his gun at Nick. "Santa. Get in here and shut the door, or I'll give these two a present they won't appreciate."

Nick stepped inside, mentally smacking himself for allowing Gwyn to separate from him during the search. He knew better, but one glance at those desperate blue eyes and he'd caved.

He was an idiot.

As if on cue, Gwyn glanced at him over her shoulder. Tiny beads of sweat dotted her skin, making strands of her long blond hair stick to her cheek.

Nick shut the door. The room seemed to be a combination break room and jewelry repair shop. A half-empty coffeepot, creamer, sugar and cups sat on the far counter along with a plate of Christmas cookies.

On the other walls were machines, tools and cleaners. None of which was useful as a weapon unless he attacked them with a coffee mug à la Jackie Chan. To the right was a closed door. Storage? A way out? He filed the information away.

Another door on the left was wide-open and seemed to be a vault of some kind. Inside the small, tight space flashlights revealed two people trying to break into the safe. Another male dressed much as the armed man. Black clothes. Leather gloves. Long blond hair tied back. The woman next to him sported a short, trendy haircut. Loads of makeup. And street clothes.

Despite the gun in her hand pegging her for a criminal, he recognized her from watching the shop all day.

She was the salesgirl.

An inside job. He knew it. Hell, anyone on the case suspected as much. They just couldn't prove it.

"We don't want any trouble," Nick said.

The gunman shifted his aim toward Nick. "I'm sure you know the routine. Hands up. Over there." He nodded toward the back wall.

Raising his hands where the man could see them, Nick walked to the back wall and pressed his lower back against the cool cement. "What's going on?"

The man took Gwyn's purse, tossed it to the floor and then nudged her with his foot. "You, too."

Nick watched as Gwyn walked toward him. Her blue eyes met his, and he saw fear in their depths. Deep, screaming fear. For him. For herself. And for the small boy who was having the most terrifying Christmas ever.

Then she took the spot next to him. "Try to stay calm," he whispered. "It'll be okay."

"I'm fine," she replied, and he realized that while she might be terrified, there was no tremble in her voice and her hands didn't shake as she squeezed his forearm before she took her place next to him on the wall.

"What now?" Gwyn asked, talking to the gunman.

"We do not need hostages," the woman in the vault said as her companion drilled into the safe.

Hostages. That meant they weren't going to be shot, at least not immediately. The tension in Nick's gut eased a notch. He could use that to his advantage. "Of course you do," he said.

"Shut up," the gunman said, cocking his gun.

"He's right," Gwyn said. "We were only supposed to be gone for ten minutes. They'll come looking for us soon, and when they don't find us…"

"Who's *they*," the girl interrupted, stepping into the room. Now that she was closer, he saw she still wore her name tag. *Marsha.* If that was her real name.

"Cops," Nick said. "Lots of cops. All looking for him," he nodded at Connor. Up until now, the boy had reminded silent, the gunman's hand still over his mouth.

"He came running in here," the girl whined. "What were we

supposed to do? Just let him go?" She glared at Connor. "This is your fault."

Next to him, Gwyn tensed and Nick groaned. Connor might not be her child but she was reacting with a woman's maternal instinct.

"His fault?" She pushed away from the wall. Nick grabbed her arm, and she shook him off. Oblivious to the guns and the danger, she marched across the room. She hesitated in front of Marsha, and for a moment, Nick thought she might go for a catfight.

Instead, she continued then stopped in front of the gunman. "He's five years old. Let him go."

"You want him?" The gunman tightened his hold.

"Yes, I do," Gwyn said, hands on her hips.

Nick cringed at her tone but kept his mouth shut. It wouldn't do to have them *both* pissing off the crooks. Let her be bad hostage. He'd be good hostage.

Until he wasn't.

He took a deep breath at the thought, eager for a little payback.

"Take him." The gunman uncovered Connor's mouth and used his knee to shove the child toward Gwyn. "Happy now?"

"Thrilled," Gwyn said, dropping to her knees and pulling Connor into her arms.

"I'm sorry," Connor said, tears tracking down his cheeks.

"You didn't do anything wrong," Gwyn said as Connor wiped his runny nose on her shoulder, making Nick cringe. Gwyn didn't flinch.

"I was scared," Connor said. "And I saw the light."

"I know. It's okay." Gwyn picked Connor up, her arms tight around him as she took her place back against the wall.

"You need to control your temper," Nick whispered. She glared at him, her blue eyes wet with tears. He thumbed one away as it slid down her cheek. "You are a dumb ass," he said, "But a brave one."

Which was admirable as long as her bravery didn't get her shot.

"Gee, thanks," Gwyn said with a sniff. "I think."

"Are you Santa?" Connor asked.

Nick shook his head. "I'm not the big guy. Just his number one helper. Santa and I are like this." He crossed his fingers.

Connor's eyes widened. "Will I be on the naughty list now, for running away?"

Nick smiled, despite the situation. "No, but they are," he said, nodding at the three crooks. "They're going to get coal in their stockings."

And a nice long stay in prison, if he had anything to do with it.

The gunman frowned. "Hey, kid, there's no such thing as Santa," he said. "It's a lie. Your parents give you the presents."

"Tucker, don't be a jerk," the safecracker said. "He's a kid, for Chrissakes. It's Christmas."

Tucker. Now that was useful information. Nick filed it away.

"Are you mental?" Tucker growled. "You said my name."

The safecracker flinched. "Sorry." He ran a hand through his hair, breaking a few strands free from the rubber band that held it back.

"Whatever. Just get back to work," Tucker said, never taking his attention from the hostages. "Stick to the plan."

"The plan? The plan is screwed. What the hell are we going to do with hostages?" the blond man argued.

Nick didn't miss the sound of Gwyn's breath catching. He touched her side, wishing he could do more. "You could let us go," he said.

"Shut. Up," Tucker replied.

"At least let them go," Nick said, not shutting up. This was his opening, and he wasn't going to let it go. Besides, he didn't think Tucker would shoot.

At least not until he had what he'd come for. Nick continued. "You can keep me. You only need one hostage, and keeping a woman and kid will just piss off the cops."

"He has a point," the blond man said. "No one likes the guys who hurt kids and women."

"How much *Oprah* have you been watching?" Tucker rolled

his eyes. "And shouldn't you both be breaking into a safe? We're wasting time."

The safecracker and Marsha went back to work.

Hell. "Just let them go," Nick said, focusing on Tucker. "I'll be the perfect hostage. Even help you carry the loot."

"Are you insane?" Gwyn broke in. "I am not leaving you here alone."

"You're right. You're not," Tucker replied. "But Stephan made a good point," he grinned, obviously aware he'd said he the other man's name and caring more for retaliation than secrecy. "Keeping a kid tends to make cops more trigger-happy than needed. He can go."

The tension in Nick's gut released yet another notch. One down. One more to go. Then they'd both be safe.

"I want to stay with you," Connor whimpered, tightening his hold on Gwyn.

Gwyn's eyes locked with Nick's as she stroked Connor's hair. *Thank you,* she mouthed. Then she kissed the top of Connor's head. "You can't stay here, sweetie. One of these people will show you which way to go, and I want you to run in that direction. Just run in a straight line until you see Glory and the policemen."

Connor buried his head in Gwyn's neck. "I can't," he sobbed. "It's dark. There're monsters."

Nick squeezed Connor's shoulder. The kid was right about one thing—there were monsters. But they were right here. "You can do this," Nick said. "I'll make sure that Santa leaves you a special present."

"And it's not dark," Gwyn chimed in. "Not at all. There are pretty red lights to lead the way. All you have to do is run."

Connor didn't move.

"Tell you what," Tucker said, "Since it's Christmas, I'll let the woman take the kid out of here."

Nick sighed in relief. Thank God. With both of them gone, he'd be free to do what was needed without fear of hurting civilians.

Tucker continued, pointing his gun at Gwyn, "But I want you to come back."

The tension in Nick's gut returned, making him groan. "Just let them go."

Tucker shook his head. "A single man makes a crap hostage. I need either the woman or the kid." He grinned. "You choose. Who stays? The woman or the kid?"

Nick frowned. Later, he'd shoot Tucker. Somewhere non-lethal that would hurt for a good, long time.

"Connor goes," Gwyn said.

"What she said," Nick agreed, knowing it was the only way to get them both out.

Tucker nodded. "She drops the kid off and gets back here in five minutes or you get shot."

Gwyn's eyes widened. "You can't kill him. Then you won't have a hostage."

"I never said kill."

If nothing else, Tucker was to the point.

Next to him, Gwyn nodded. "Deal."

Hearing her conviction, Nick wanted to shake her. Hell, she knew he was a cop. And she was savvy. Smart. She should know that he didn't *want* her gone. He *needed* her gone.

"You better get moving," Tucker said. "Countdown starts now."

"Do not come back," Nick said, not caring who heard him.

"I can't do that," Gwyn said. With Connor in her arms, she rushed toward the door, stopping long enough to flash one last look of desperation at Nick. "I'm sorry." Then she was gone, leaving Nick alone with Tucker and his crew.

"You better hope she's fast," Tucker said, keeping his gun on Nick.

Nick didn't bother to answer. He didn't want her to be fast. He wanted her to run away and stay away.

He'd been shot before—his thigh ached with phantom pain at the memory—and he wasn't eager to take another bullet, but it was better than watching Gwyn take one when this job was over and Tucker killed them both.

Chapter 5

Five minutes.

Carrying Connor, Gwyn sprinted through the mall, feeling as if she were part of the most sadistic game show ever created.

Beat the clock and win fabulous prizes. Money. A car. *Nick's life.*

Ahead of her, the hallway brightened as she grew closer to the south entrance and her sister. Not much farther. Her breath hitched in her chest as she passed a bookstore.

"Look, sweetie," she huffed. "We're almost there."

Connor remained quiet, his face buried against her neck. She'd hoped that once they were closer to safety he'd relax because as bad as she felt for the little guy, she couldn't go with him. Not the whole way. If she did, Nick's men would never let her leave. And then Tucker would shoot Nick, and while he said it wouldn't be a kill shot, she didn't believe him. Tucker looked like the kind of man who enjoyed death.

The thought left a bitter taste in her mouth, and she sped up. That wasn't going to happen. She'd make sure of it.

Three storefronts later marked the end of her run. Carefully, she pried Connor's arms away from her neck and set him on his feet.

"Where is everyone?" he asked, his hand in hers.

Squatting down, Gwyn touched his cheek. "They're right around the corner, but you have to go on without me, sweetie."

He pushed himself back into her arms. "I'm scared. Go with me."

Gwyn squeezed her eyes shut. Hating Tucker. Hating herself. "No, sweetie. You have to go," Gwyn said, prying him off of her and feeling like the cruelest person ever born. "I have to go help Nick."

"The number one helper?" His tone perked up.

"Yes." She wished she had more time to explain. To talk Connor into doing what she needed. But she only had two minutes to get back to Tucker and the store. Turning the boy, she guided him around the corner. "Run," she said, and headed back into the dark, ignoring the cries echoing behind her.

Her heart pounding with both effort and fear, Gwyn pushed herself and arrived at the jewelry store in record time. She pelted through the door into the back room.

Tucker's gun remained pointed at Nick. "Welcome back."

"My pleasure," Gwyn snapped, trying to catch her breath.

His back against the wall, Nick frowned at her. She shrugged. She knew he was pissed that she'd come back, but he'd do the same for her. Besides, only cowards left someone else to pay for their mistakes. She might suck at a lot of things—love, work and cooking—but she wasn't a coward and didn't plan to start now.

Tucker opened the heavy door on the right. "Both of you. In here."

Gwyn glanced at Nick. He nodded, and she walked into the room with him and Tucker following.

As big as the outer room, file cabinets lined the far wall. Otherwise, it was empty.

"The light stays on or the next time I walk in, I'll be shooting," Tucker said, shutting the door and locking them in.

Behind her, she heard Nick close the distance between them, fury in his footsteps. She forced herself to remain still. Even if he wasn't a cop, she suspected he was the kind of man who was used to others doing what he said.

But she wasn't the kind of person who obeyed directives that got people shot. Still, she dreaded the lecture, even as she knew it was coming from the moment she left with Connor.

"Gwyn." He said her name like a sigh, his breath warm against her neck.

Determined to remain stoic, she allowed herself to shut her eyes.

"Thank you," he whispered.

Gwyn's eyes popped open. "What?"

He sighed again, but this time there was nothing but pure exasperation in the sound. "Are you really going to make me say it twice?"

Curiosity drove her to turn and meet his eyes. "I don't get it. I thought you'd be pissed."

His right brow arched upward. "Oh, I am."

Then she saw the fury in his gaze. Nope, he wasn't lying about that. He was totally pissed. But beneath the fury was something else. What, she wasn't sure, but it was quieter than the anger, and the fact she couldn't read it scared the hell out of her. Hell, if she had to admit it, Nick scared her. He was the unknown and unexpected, and in her line of work, those two factors rarely added up to a good thing.

He continued, "You're a hindrance here. You know it. I know it."

"I've never been known for playing well with others," she said, sounding more glib than she intended. She didn't feel a whit of remorse for doing the right thing instead of the smart thing.

Nick rolled his eyes. "But I also know that coming back to be a hostage wasn't easy, and when it comes down to it, I don't like the thought of being shot." He smoothed a strand of hair from her cheek, shaking his head. "Besides, I can't do much about it, can I?"

Gwyn shrugged, trying to ignore the warmth of his touch. "Not unless you have a gun tucked in your pocket."

He tensed. The reaction lasted for less than a second but that was all she needed to know that he was armed, even if he didn't want to admit it. She might be trained as a P.I., but it was her innate skill to read people that made her a *good* P.I.

Well, read people that weren't family or lovers. Once she added emotions to the mix, her skills tanked.

Nick relaxed, his hand lingering by her ear. "I need you to make me a promise."

Here it came. "Let me guess," Gwyn said, flashing him a smile that she knew was anything but sincere. "Stay out of trouble. Play the damsel in distress? Let you do all the rescuing?"

Once again he tensed, but this time she knew it was because she'd struck a nerve.

"I'm not asking you to play the damsel in distress. I'm asking you to let me handle this."

"Because you're the professional?"

He ran both hands through his hair, gripping the short strands. "*Of course,* because I'm the professional."

Time to fill him in on what was what. "Nick, I'm a private investigator. I'm a professional, too. I can handle this."

He shook his head, hands still on top of his head, fingers woven together. "A P.I.? That means insurance fraud and tailing men who define faithfulness as not getting caught. That does not mean you're prepared for this."

She couldn't deny his assessment, but the way he said it made her sound *weak.* And she wasn't weak. Not now. Now ever.

Unlacing his hands, Nick crossed his arms over is chest. "When was the last time you had to shoot a man?"

Gwyn crossed her arms, mirroring his actions. If she gave ground now, she'd never recover. "Never and you know it, but I'm savvy and smart when it comes to getting out of sketchy situations."

"As demonstrated by your decision to come back here," Nick shot back.

So much for his thanks. "And saved your butt."

Nick's hands shot out, grabbing her before she could react. His hands tightened on her arms, and his dark brows drew downward. "Yes, and I appreciate it, but this is serious, and we're not safe just because they locked us in the back room. They are killers, and when they get what they want we are dead."

Worry cast shadows across his face, softening the frustration that radiated from him in waves. "Is that what you want your sister to remember for the holidays? That Christmas Eve was the day she lost you?"

She hadn't allowed herself to think about her sister, but Nick gave her no choice. Gwyn swallowed hard, her eyes filling with angry, desperate tears as she thought about her sister waiting. Wondering. "You're an ass," she said, the words catching in her throat.

Nick's eyes and grip softened. "I'm trying to make a point."

"Consider it made," she said, wiping her eyes before a tear could make its way down her cheek.

"Please don't cry," he said, pulling her close.

Gwyn knew she should push away, but found herself burying her head on his chest instead, accepting the unexpected comfort.

Glory.

What if she never saw her again? The thought was unbearable. And she knew her sister—if Tucker killed her, Glory would replay the entire day in her head. Wonder what she might have done differently. Take on a guilt she didn't deserve.

The tears came despite Gwyn's desire to keep them inside, and she twisted her hands in Nick's shirt.

"It's okay," Nick whispered.

Not yet. But it would be. Gwyn took a deep breath to compose herself and then let it out. Then another. After the third, the tears stopped, and she raised her face to Nick's. "I still think you're an ass."

He smiled down at her and brushed a final tear away with the pad of his thumb. "It'll be okay."

"Promise me," she said. "Promise me we'll get out of here."

His smile died and his gaze flickered down to her mouth then back to her eyes. "I promise."

He said it like he meant it. Like he believed it. But she knew better. "Liar." Rising on her toes, she brushed his lips with hers, knowing it was inappropriate, the worst timing in the world, and not caring. If just for a few seconds, she needed to feel safe, and there was no place safer than Nick's arms, even if he didn't know it. Even if he didn't care.

Nick tightened his hold on her waist and lifted her up off her feet. The tip of his tongue tickled her lower lip.

New Year's Resolution be dammed. This wasn't a date. Besides, if it were, it was the worst one ever. She opened to him, her mouth pressed against his as they explored each other until the only sound she heard was their breathing and the only thing she felt was his touch.

She wasn't sure how much time had passed when Nick set her back on her feet, breaking the kiss and ending the moment. "We should figure out a strategy if I plan to keep that promise," he said.

He sounded as if nothing had happened, but the red tint to his face said otherwise. She considered giving him a bad time, but he was right, they did need to figure out their next step. Kissing could wait. "We should," she agreed. Putting some needed space between them, she resisted the urge to take refuge in the safety of his arms. After all, it was just an illusion. They weren't safe and wouldn't be until they escaped. "What next?"

Nick scrubbed the back of his neck. "I'll be damned if I can see an exit other than the door—not unless you can fit through that vent."

She followed his gaze to a vent that was, perhaps, no more than ten inches in either height or width. "Connor couldn't fit through that."

She clasped her hands in front of her. "So, any ideas on

weapons?" She wondered if he'd own up to carrying the gun now that they'd kissed. Though she doubted it. Nick was a compartmentalize kind of guy. Kissing was kissing. Trusting her to know he carried a gun was something else entirely.

Before she could find out, the door swung open, and Tucker filled in the doorway, gun in one hand and her cell phone in the other.

He tossed the phone to Gwyn. "You have a call."

She caught it midair. "Excuse me?"

"Your sister."

She didn't want to know how he knew that. "What do you want me to do?"

"The cops are outside the mall, and we want to make sure they stay there. Have her tell them to stay back or someone gets shot. Keep it short."

Gwyn nodded and dialed Glory. Her sister answered in seconds. "Gwyn?"

"It's me," Gwyn confirmed.

"Oh my God, are you okay?" Glory asked. Gwyn could only imagine the panic her sister must feel.

In the background, she heard the chatter increase as the police realized who it was on the other end of Glory's call.

"I want to listen." Tucker tilted his head so he could hear her. His gun pressed into her side and one eye stayed on Nick.

"We're fine," Gwyn said. "But I can't talk long."

"Hold on," Glory said. "The sergeant wants to speak to you."

Tucker jammed the gun harder into her side.

"No. Just you," Gwyn said, "No one else."

Glory hesitated, and both could hear someone telling her what to say. "Okay. What do they want?"

"For the cops to stay away."

"That's all?"

"That's it. So far," Gwyn said.

"I'd feel better if there were more," Glory said. "Demands or something."

Gwyn empathized with how helpless Glory must feel. If there were demands, at least she could act. Feel as if the situation were moving forward. "Sorry," Gwyn said. "That's all they want."

Glory sighed into the receiver. "At least you're with a cop. That makes me feel better."

Gwyn winced as Glory finished the sentence. Before she could respond, Tucker grabbed the phone, snapped it shut, and pointed the gun at Nick. "You're a cop?"

Chapter 6

"**Y**ou fire that weapon and every policeman outside this mall will be in here before you can get fifty yards." Nick remained as calm as possible despite the fact his mind raced, seeking any possible avenue of escape. Unfortunately, all scenarios ended up with both him and Gwyn dead. The attempt to kill them was going to be made—there was no doubt about that—but not yet. Tucker wasn't ready.

"We're in the middle of the mall, and they're outside. They won't hear it," Tucker said, hand steady and finger still on the trigger.

"Trust me, they're listening," Nick said. "In fact, they're waiting for an excuse to come storming in here."

Tucker's hand lowered a millimeter.

"And then you'll never get the diamonds," Nick continued, trying to convince Tucker that waiting was in the thief's best interest.

"Good point," Tucker said. "Now put your weapon on the floor."

Dammit. Tucker wasn't a fool. He'd known that but still, one could hope. Nick glanced at Gwyn. There were no more tears. No regret. Instead, she glared at Tucker, her mouth flattened in anger. Good. They'd need that.

Nick took out his Sig, set it on the floor and kicked it toward the thief.

"Pants off." Tucker waved the weapon toward Nick's Santa pants.

"Right," Nick replied, keeping his temper under control, telling himself that the more he cooperated, the faster Tucker would leave them alone so he could focus on escape. Shrugging the suspenders off his shoulders, Nick let the oversize Santa pants fall to his ankles and stepped out of them.

"Over here."

Nick kicked them over—glad he'd kept his jeans and T-shirt on beneath the Santa suit.

Taking the pants in one hand, Tucker shook them and Nick's radio fell out. He slid the radio into the other room and tossed the pants after them. "Marsha," he called behind him. "Get in here."

"What?" The salesgirl walked in, hands on her hips. "Stephan's almost done."

"Frisk him," Tucker said, nodding at Nick. "He's a cop."

"Great," Marsha growled. Walking over to Nick, she ran her hands over his torso, up and down his legs and even taking the time to give his crotch a squeeze. Amateurish but just as effective. "He's clean." She rose with a snort of disgust and headed back to the other room. "God, I hate this job."

"Kidnapping, hurting kids and potential jail time? What's not to love," Gwyn chimed in.

Nick winced at the cattiness in her tone. Her anger would be useful only if she could control it.

Marsha stopped midstep, but Tucker grabbed her arm, handed her Gwyn's phone and propelled her out of the room. "Don't bother. We need to get moving before the cops get brave."

Following her, he shut the door, locking them back in. The sound of Stephan's drilling filtered under the door, their one

gauge of how much time they had before Tucker decided he
didn't need them alive anymore.

"Did you notice she said 'almost done,'" Gwyn asked. "We
don't have much time."

Nick scrubbed at his chin, running more scenarios for possible salvation. There weren't many. With no cover in the room,
Gwyn was a potential target no matter what he did.

He glanced down at her and wondered what it would be like
to be with her in the real world. Typically, he preferred buxom
brunettes with more curves. Professionals who found his work
fascinating but who had no desire to hold a gun or capture the
bad guy. Women with an Audrey Hepburn demureness. Not a
Xena wannabe.

Hell, blond, mouthy, private detectives weren't even on his
radar. But someone with Gwyn's passion and compassion
needed to live. Someone who kissed like her needed to see
Christmas morning.

And he needed to know what he'd been missing by limiting
his dating pool.

"What are you grinning about?" Gwyn asked, eyebrows
high. "We're going to die soon."

"No, we're not," Nick said. Placing a hand on either side of
her face, he kissed her hard and quick. "I promised you we'd
be okay, and I plan to keep that promise."

Gwyn touched her mouth but didn't respond.

So, kisses could shut her up? Nick filed the information
away for future use.

"How?"

She was going to hate the solution, but he didn't see another
one. Not considering what they had to work with. "I want you
to take as much cover as you can—"

"Where would that be?" She pushed the oversized filing
cabinet. It didn't budge. "Behind these?"

"Get behind the door and hunker down," Nick said, ignoring her sarcasm. He was tempted to turn off the lights, but if

he did, Tucker would come in shooting. "I'll stand on the other side and take Tucker out as he comes in."

"That's the plan?" Gwyn said, smoothing her hair back and looking at him as if he had the IQ of a rock and the experience of a rookie.

Nick's face heated at the criticism, and the reason he dated brunettes that didn't want to catch bad guys came rushing back—they didn't question his judgment in critical situations. "And then you shut the door and lock it before the others enter."

She didn't seem impressed. "Can you do better?" he asked.

"Yes." She took a deep breath. "I concede that you need to take on Tucker. Not me."

"Gee thanks," Nick snapped.

Gwyn shrugged. "But he'll be ready for that. He's not an idiot. We need a distraction."

"And that would be you?" Nick asked, following what he knew was going to be a train wreck of an idea.

"Do we have anything else?" Gwyn challenged.

"He will shoot you before you can do a damned thing," Nick said.

Gwyn brushed her hair back again. "Trust me, I can keep him occupied for a few seconds, and that should give you time to disarm him."

"How?"

"I'll be topless," Gwyn explained. "He'll never expect that, and I've been told they're fairly spectacular."

He didn't doubt the latter, but even so, her suggestion had to be the most harebrained idea he'd ever heard of, and it was also the most likely to get her shot. "I appreciate the commitment, but it's too risky."

Gwyn's mouth flattened again.

"I'm not going to argue," Nick said.

Her mouth relaxed. "Okay."

Lying again. When this was over, he'd have to talk to her about that.

The outer room grew silent. No drilling. No conversation.

And no more time to convince Gwyn to listen to his better, more experienced judgment.

Their time was up.

Hide behind the door? The thought of watching Nick take on Tucker without backup made Gwyn as nauseous as when she'd lost Connor. But she also knew that Nick would never let her help.

Not willingly.

And they only had seconds before all hell broke loose.

The thieves' conversation filtered through the walls. In her mind's eye, Gwyn could see them emptying the safe, discussing who got what and who killed who. Nick motioned for her to hide. Gwyn took her place, knowing he wouldn't do the same until she complied. With one hand, she unhooked her bra.

Nick glared at her.

"I get hives when I'm nervous," she whispered, scratching her skin.

He shook his head but didn't argue.

Hands on the hem of her sweater, Gwyn stared at the handle of the door, heart beating in her ears.

The brass handle turned. The door moved inward.

And in one, swift movement, she yanked her sweater and bra over her head, tossed them to the floor and stepped into Tucker's direct view as the door completed its swing.

For a heartbeat, Tucker gaped at her. Another beat went by.

Then Nick was on him. Grabbing the gun barrel, he pulled the weapon aside. In seconds, the men were grappling for control. Gwyn rushed forward, slammed the door shut, and braced herself against it. Seconds crawled by, and she realized that no one was trying to enter. There was no shot. No pounding on the door. Not even a half-hearted shout.

They'd left their companion to take the fall.

Nick and Tucker fell to the ground. Equally matched in height, weight and drive to win, they rolled across the floor.

Keeping clear of the fight, Gwyn waited for any opportunity to help. The men rolled toward her, ending up almost at her feet. Aiming for Tucker's kidney, Gwyn lashed out with her foot but the men rolled again, and she made contact with Nick's ribs.

"Sorry!"

He didn't seem to notice as they each continued to fight for dominance.

Gwyn bit her lip, watching for opportunity. The fight had to end and soon. The longer it lasted, the more chances there were for Nick to be hurt. The men rolled again. This time, Nick ended up on top, straddling his opponent, hands on Tucker's forearms.

Bad leverage, Gwyn knew, and impossible for him to get the gun that way.

But not for her.

Raising her foot, she caught Nick's eye. He nodded and she stomped on Tucker's wrist with all her strength. The thief screamed, and his hand opened, fingers in spasm. Gwyn dropped to her knees, grabbing the weapon before he could recover. "Freeze," she shouted, pointing it at his head.

Nick rolled away and to his feet in a single motion.

Tucker lay on the floor, grasping his wrist and moaning.

She hoped she broke it.

"You okay?" Nick asked, breathing heavy and coming around to stand at her side.

"Good. You?" Gwyn kept her eyes on Tucker.

"We caught one of the Christmas Bandits and you're half naked," he said, sizing her up. "Merry Christmas to me." Taking her elbow, he helped her to her feet.

A self-conscious flush worked its way from her head to her feet, then grew deeper as she realized there was no way to hide her embarrassment. "Nice to see almost getting killed hasn't killed your observational skills," she said, handing him the gun so she could retrieve her sweater.

"It's been a good day," Nick said.

Slipping her sweater on, she held out her bra. "Should we tie him up?"

"Do it," Nick said. He poked Tucker with his feet. "Turn over. Hands behind your back."

"No," Tucker shot back, defiant.

Gwyn shook her head. What a moron. "Nick might be hindered by the law not to hurt you but I'm not."

He rolled over.

"Thank God for Victoria's Secret," Gwen said, tying his hands behind his back. "Now let's get the hell out of here."

Nick shook his head. "I'm not leaving him."

Alarms went off in Gwyn's head. Nick was a by-the-book kind of guy and as far as she knew, staying was anything but that. "He's not going anywhere," she said.

"I don't care. I am not taking any chances on him getting away. Just go get backup. I'll wait."

She understood his reasoning, but still, it didn't seem right. "Why not take Tucker with us?" she asked.

"Do you think he'll do that willingly?"

He had a point. "Okay." Cupping his face in her hands, she kissed him as hard as he'd kissed her.

When she pulled away, his eyes were open and still on Tucker, but she was sure the grin on his face was for her and her alone.

Smartass.

She let Nick take the lead when they opened the door, but the room was empty. Marsha and Stephan were gone. But not long gone though, she realized, hearing their footsteps heading away from the store. Cowards.

"You're safe," he said. "Just hurry."

She hesitated in the doorway, still hating the thought of leaving him alone. "I'll be right back," she said.

"We'll be waiting," Nick replied.

Gwyn trotted toward the south entrance. Damn, if Nick was hot before this, saving her life and holding a weapon on the bad guy made him hotter.

Her face heated at the memory of his mouth on hers.

Behind her, a thud sounded down the empty, wide corridor.

Gwyn stopped. Were the others coming back to save their friend? If so, they'd kill Nick. Adrenaline surged through her as she sprinted back to the store. Slowing as she grew close, she watched, waiting for movement.

Seconds later, she spotted a shadow emerging, and her breath caught in her chest. Tucker? Had he somehow managed to free himself? And where the hell was Nick? She hadn't heard gun shots, but that didn't mean something hadn't gone wrong.

The dark figure stepped into the red lighting and Gwyn frowned. Not Tucker.

Nick.

Chapter 7

He was going after the others.

"He's a dead man," Gwyn whispered, hurrying after Nick, pissed that she fell for his story.

Odds were Stephan and Marsha were well on their way to freedom, but it was also possible that Nick would catch up to them. Two against one if he did. She didn't like the odds.

Ahead of her, Nick rounded a corner and disappeared from sight. She moved faster. Luckily, she could lose him for only so long, but not being able to see him—to ensure he was alive and breathing—made her pulse race.

A slamming door echoed through the silent mall, "It's not my fault." Marsha's distinctive whine made Gwyn pause. "You act like I don't want to get away. He didn't tell me, either."

Gwyn smiled. Apparently, Tucker hadn't told them the escape route. Normally, control freaks made her nuts, but in this case, she appreciated Tucker's need to run the show.

First, she had to catch up to Nick, but as she rounded the

corner, Nick was nowhere in sight, "Dammit," she muttered under her breath. Where had he gone?

Seconds later, a hand went over her mouth, and someone jerked her into an alcove. Panic and instinct working in tandem, she jammed her elbow into her attacker, connecting with his ribs. His grip loosened, and she went limp so she could slip downward and escape.

But he tightened hold before she could drop more than a few inches and killed the momentum she needed to make another attack.

"Are you insane," a familiar voice whispered in her ear.

Nick. She bit his hand, getting just enough flesh to pinch. It might be a small bite, but they hurt oh-so-much more, and he deserved at least that for scaring the hell out of her.

He let go.

"You couldn't just say, 'Psst! In here,'" she hissed, jerking out of his grasp.

"And you couldn't just do as I asked? For once," Nick replied.

"Not when you're being an idiot."

"If you'd gone to get help, like I asked, we'd have backup by now," Nick said with a sigh.

"You could also be dead by now," Gwyn said.

"Hardly."

Irritation kept Gwyn's pulse pounding. "One, you don't know where the other two are." She ticked the reasons off on her fingers, even though he couldn't see her. "Two, there are two of them. Both armed."

"I'm not sure about Marsha," Nick said.

Gwyn ignored him. "Three, it only takes a few seconds for you to get shot, which brings us to four." She held her fingers up, wiggling them. "You are not invincible, and if you died because I left you with no backup…" The thought made her want to both cry and pound Nick for not understanding her fear.

"That's five," Nick said, as he traced a tender path up her arm, across her shoulder and stopping to cup her cheek.

He did understand. "Jerk," Gwyn said, trying to mean it.

"I know," Nick replied, stroking her skin. "But I feel the same way. If something happened to you, I'd never forgive myself."

The sweetness of the comment surprised her, but Gwyn pushed the warm-fuzzy feeling aside. They had two more thieves to catch. "We should get moving."

"Not yet." Nick pressed one of the guns into her hands. "And take this. It has a full clip. One in the chamber."

"Thanks." She tucked the gun into the back of her jeans. "What are we waiting for?"

"For them to make more noise and give us some indication of their location," Nick said. "I want to catch them, but I don't want either of us shot. So, we wait. Once we know where they are, you head back."

As if. But Gwyn knew better than to argue. With fingers crossed, she nodded and leaned against the wall, knowing he was too preoccupied to catch the lie.

"There's more to the shelter kids than you said," Nick said after a few minutes.

Gwyn's brows shot up, not startled by his voice so close to her ear but at the unexpected, out-of-the-blue comment. "Why do you keep doing that?"

"Doing what?"

"Blurting out random questions at the most inappropriate times," she whispered.

"They're not random," Nick replied.

She waved this off. She should have known as much, but she wasn't going to offer her life story because his cop instincts told her there was something in her past worth knowing.

"I've seen social workers who work with the shelters," he said, obviously ignoring her discomfort. "They're good, don't get me wrong. But taking kids to see Santa? That's above the call of duty."

Gwyn shifted from one foot to another. "My sister is a good-hearted person. Nothing more."

"I don't doubt it, but still." Nick grew closer in the darkness. "Most people donate toys or clothes. Not time."

Gwyn crossed her arms over her chest, trying to keep both

Nick and her memories at bay. "What does it matter? Why do you care?"

Running his hand over her arm, Nick uncrossed her arms and wound his fingers with hers. "I just do. So talk."

Talk about one of the worst times in her life? Now? "I can't," she replied, struggling to get the words out of her throat.

"Talk to me," Nick insisted. "We have nothing else to do. Not yet."

"Shouldn't we be listening?"

"I can do both."

Gwyn squeezed her eyes shut, the past playing across her eyelids like an old movie. "When I was ten, my mother left my father on Christmas Eve. We spent the next six months living in shelters while my mother tried to find work so she could take care of us."

Silence. Had she said too much? Was he freaked out by her past?

"Did she?" Nick asked after a few moments, his tone hopeful.

Gwyn shook her head, wishing the ending was a happy one. Something one watched on Lifetime. "No. She found another husband."

Allen. A lawyer who was just as bad as their father. Granted, he didn't beat them with belts. Words were his whips. He called them names. Cheated on their mother and then denied it, calling her crazy and irrational.

Gwyn stayed until Glory was old enough to leave. Then they both moved out one weekend, begging their mother to go with them. She refused, and Glory almost stayed behind, as well—only Gwyn's plea that she couldn't afford the apartment by herself forced her sister to follow.

"He sucked, too, didn't he?" Nick asked, reading her silence.

"Yes."

"It happens, you know," Nick said, kissing the knuckles. "People get beat down long enough and it begins to feel 'normal.' It's what they know. So it's what they look for in their next relationship."

Gwyn crossed her arms over her chest, trying to keep hold

"I know. Glory said the same thing."

"Smart woman, your sister," Nick said.

"Straight A's," Gwyn said.

"How about you? Any college?"

"Tried it," she said. "It wasn't for me." After she'd left school, here had been an endless parade of administrative assistant jobs that bored her to tears. Then five years ago, she'd found her calling as a P.I., and had been content—until just a few months ago.

"And I liked being a P.I....for a while," she confessed.

"Burnout happens," Nick said.

Burnout or something more. Something deeper. She wasn't sure but she knew that now wasn't the time for a therapy session. "Yeah. Burnout." She leaned her forehead against his chest.

Murmuring made her straighten and adrenaline surged through her, transforming warmth into heat. "Is it them?"

"Who else," Nick said. He poked his head into the main walkway. She followed.

The voices were faint and far away and the couple was out of sight. "I heard Marsha say that Tucker hadn't told them the escape route," Gwyn whispered.

"Not a surprise," Nick said. "Now, go." He stepped into the walkway. Gwyn followed, a few steps behind.

He stopped midstep and hunkered low. "Dammit, Gwyn. This is not the time."

Frustration and worry darkened his eyes, and while it tugged at her heart, it didn't sway her one iota. "This is exactly the time," she whispered. "Either I go or neither of us goes."

Nick hesitated, turmoil replacing worry and then morphing into acceptance. "For now," he finally said.

Not what she wanted but it was better than fighting while the crooks escaped. "For now," she agreed.

Stepping around the red beams of the emergency lights, they made their way forward, using kiosks as cover when possible and keeping low.

Gwyn's heart pounded in her ears, and she was sure Stephan and Marsha could hear the thudding. Ahead of her, Nick motioned for her to wait.

Did he see them? There were no voices now for her to follow, and he had the better vantage. He gestured for her to move again.

The familiar squeal of a metal gate rising made Gwyn freeze. Nick dropped to the ground.

Fear threaded her spine.

It was Tucker. He'd escaped.

Nick frowned. "I should have shot him," he said under his breath.

"You're not that kind of cop," Gwyn said.

She was right, but at times like this—when her body trembled and he knew it had nothing to do with being cold—he wished he were.

He had no doubt that Tucker would search for his cohorts since they had the diamonds. So he and Gwyn didn't have long before the thief would spot them, and he wanted to remain unseen. As long as Tucker was free, he could use the gunman to lead him to the other two thieves.

But there was no kiosk to duck into, no hallway in sight and nothing to hide behind. The only cover was a wooden bench back by a giant planter full of ferns a few feet away.

"Under here," he said, dragging Gwyn down beside him. Lying on his back, he slid under the bench, keeping his arms above his head and as free as possible.

"This is going to be tight," Gwyn whispered, but she squeezed in on top of him.

Tight was an understatement, and he was glad she wasn't an Amazon. She shifted against him, an unintentional full-body rub that under any other circumstances would demand reciprocation.

"Lumpy but cozy," she whispered. "And for the record, I usually at least demand dinner and a movie before we get to this."

"I might be able to scare up a Wetzel's Pretzel."

"You won't even get to second base with a pretzel," Gwyn whispered.

Nick shifted his hips. "I think I might already be at third."

Her cheek pressed against his, he felt her smile. Footsteps sounded, and they both froze. The quips died.

Tucker's tall frame came into view, his hands still bound behind his back.

Nick's hand tightened around his weapon, ready to open fire if necessary. Gwyn's chest stilled as she held her breath, waiting. He saw her hand tense, her finger resting alongside the trigger.

Then the thief was past them. Between the dim lighting and his obvious desire to catch up with his companions, he hadn't even glanced in their direction. With the sound of Tucker's footfalls diminishing, Gwyn wiggled free of their shelter. She rolled to her knees, gun at the ready and covering him as he slid out from under the bench. "We should hurry," she said. "Once he tells them the exit, we'll never catch them."

Nick took in her stance—the way she held her weapon, her calm eagerness and the controlled hyperalertness.

Still female but of the more lethal variety.

She was right. If needed, she could be backup.

Even as the thought flickered through his mind, he pushed it away. He'd been an idiot for her already. Let her convince him to let her tag along. He wasn't going to walk that path again.

She was a civilian. And not even the thought of catching Christmas Bandits could make him put her in danger again.

He shook his head. "I can see you're good, but it's time for you to go back. There is no *we*. Not here. Not now."

Chapter 8

"No we?" Gwyn asked. For the past hour or so, there had been nothing but the "we." Nothing but them—working together and fighting at each other's side.

We.

One side of Nick's mouth curved in a small half smile. "Well, at least not when it comes to taking on the bad guys."

Gwyn froze as a band of butterflies broke out in her stomach, and for a moment, she didn't know how to respond. Did he mean it or was he just saying anything in hopes that she'd cooperate and remain behind while he took on three armed gunmen alone?

She pressed a hand against her stomach, willing the butterflies to go away. The other corner of his mouth curved upward, as well.

The butterflies multiplied.

Damn, it was tempting. *We.* Could there be a *we* for them? Maybe. Perhaps.

Even if it were true, that was in the future—if they both lived. She sighed. Butterflies or no, she wasn't wavering in her decision. If he wanted Tucker and his crew, he was taking her. He needed someone to guard his back and there was no one else. "You can argue if you want, but you're just losing time and letting them get away."

Nick's flash of smile disappeared, taking her butterflies with it.

"Then we both stay," he said. "I won't put you in danger."

Gwyn rolled her eyes. Noble as hell and what she expected. As if that would work.

"I'm going. You can do what you want," she said, heading in the direction Tucker had run. She prayed Nick followed her. If she thought it was nuts for him to take on the thieves, it was a suicide mission for her. She was trained to watch. To take pictures and not get caught. To act as a backup. Not point.

That was Nick's forte.

She didn't slow as she squinted into red-lit darkness to find Tucker. Already a number of stores away, Tucker was moving faster than she'd thought, especially considering his hands were still bound.

Nick paced her, not saying a word.

Was he going to call her bluff? "Stay behind me and do *everything* I tell you to," he whispered, taking the lead. "Unless you want to challenge me on that, as well."

Gwyn snickered. "I'm good."

Two flashlight beams appeared, followed by angry tones and the occasional swear. Tucker had found his cohorts and wasn't too pleased they'd left him behind.

Gwyn tightened her grip on the gun. He'd be even less pleased with jail.

Nick pulled her behind a planter.

Kneeling on the floor, Gwyn strained to hear the three, but now that they were past the bickering, it was impossible to make out the conversation. She peered around the foliage and watched as the thieves walked across the corridor, skirted a kiosk and disappeared into a hallway a few stores down. "They're on the move," she whispered.

Nick motioned for her to follow but when they reached the side corridor, the three were gone. "Where the hell did they go?" Gwyn muttered, the gun held barrel up and close to her chest.

Nick edged his way into the darkness. "There's got to be a doorway. Feel along the wall. Be careful and be quiet."

As if she needed to be told. Taking the opposite side, Gwyn walked through the dark, dragging her hand along the wall. Within seconds, she hit the frame of a door. "Got it," she whispered, her body shaking with adrenaline.

Two shots rang out from the other side of the door, and Nick dragged her to the floor.

Flattened on the cold tile, Gwyn waited for shouting. Gunshots. The door to open. Something. But there was no more noise.

"You okay?" Nick whispered.

"I'm fine. What was that about?"

"One less person to share with."

"No honor among thieves," Gwyn said.

"Not when you have hundreds of thousands in diamonds involved," Nick said, helping her to her feet. "Wait here."

She sighed. He just couldn't let it go. "No."

A dark shadow in the almost pitch-black hallway, he pulled her close. Gwyn didn't struggle. She knew it was a tactic to soften her, but she didn't care. Not that it would work, but she could at least enjoy the moment of silence and safety.

"I've humored the hell out of you," he said, and kissed the top of her head. "But someone just died, Gwyn. This is as real as it gets. If you go, I'll be focused on keeping you safe, not doing my job."

"You need backup," she argued, hating his logic.

"There are only two now. Maybe even one. They don't know I'm coming. I can handle that. I don't need you there. I need you here. Safe."

For the first time since they'd begun their argument over her role, she heard finality in his tone. He meant it. He wasn't going to let her go. Not now.

But she couldn't let it go. Not that easily. Not when it felt like fear was winning. "How about I wait at the doorway," she offered, galled by the compromise that came from her mouth.

Nick sighed, his breath warm against her scalp. "Can you do that? Just wait?"

"Yes."

His fingers in her hair, he tilted her mouth up to his. The kiss was brief and quick, but she felt the concern behind it, as well as the pledge of more. *If* they lived. "Stay behind me," he said. "And remember your promise."

Slowly, he opened the door. Silence and the same red security lights greeted them but nothing else. No Tucker. No crew. Just the lights and a stairway that ended in a hallway that stretched outward and away from the mall.

"Maintenance corridor," Nick said. "Probably goes to an outlying building of some sort."

"That explains why they seemed so sure they could escape," Gwyn said.

"Why Tucker seemed so sure." Nick cocked his gun and met her eyes. "Wait."

"A promise is a promise," she said, still hating it.

Without another word or a backward glance, Nick hurried down the stairs and disappeared.

Gwyn shifted from foot to foot, forcing herself remain behind. After a minute, she counted each foot shift. If he didn't come back by the time she reached five-hundred, she'd follow him and screw her promise.

At one-hundred fifty, a shot rang out.

Every nerve in Gwyn's body spiked, and she pelted down the stairs, taking two at a time. Barely breaking stride when she reached the bottom, she ran down the corridor. Lined with electrical conduits and a large pipe, it appeared empty. By the time she reached a junction almost fifty feet away, she had her panic under control.

Slowing, she took a deep breath. Nick needed her alert. In control. Not racing around like a heroine who was too stupid to live.

"I'm coming," she muttered as she stuck her head around the next corner, prepared for the worst.

Twenty feet away, a body lay in the middle of the corridor. "Nick." Pulse pounding, she ran to him. "Please, don't be Nick."

Her pulse slowed. At her feet lay Stephan—his eyes blank, mouth open and two gunshot wounds that left his chest a study in blood. Marsha was nowhere to be seen, which meant she was with Tucker. She'd thought Marsha was Stephan's girl.

It seemed both she and Stephan were wrong.

Despite the disturbing scene, Gwyn couldn't scare up a shred of remorse. He might have been betrayed, but that didn't make him one of the good guys. Stepping over the body, she continued down the corridor. It ended in an open doorway. Cautiously, Gwyn peered inside.

The room wasn't huge, but it appeared to contain every electrical conduit and pipe for the water system for the mall. She guessed that if the power were on, it would be one of the loudest rooms in the building. As it was, it was silent. The quiet, combined with the shadows, reminded her of a horror film—the kind where a masked, ax-wielding maniac chased down half-naked teenagers.

"Give yourself up," she heard Nick shout. "You're pinned."

There was no answer. Gwyn followed the voice and spotted her partner on the other side of the room, taking cover behind a large pipe.

"What's wrong?" Nick continued, "Not feeling chatty now that we're both armed?"

Gwyn knew what he as doing—trying to goad Tucker into giving up his location. A good idea, and there wasn't much else Nick could do considering the circumstances, but she sensed Tucker wasn't the type to fall for such an obvious ploy.

Wherever Tucker hid, he wasn't within eyesight. "Nick," she called his name in a stage whisper.

He jumped. "Is this how you keep a promise?" he hissed.

Gwyn shrugged, knowing he was pissed and not caring.

"Stay there," he said. Firing into the dark, he sprinted across the walkway. Shots rang out in return, but by then, he was at her side.

Nick frowned, the red lighting etching his face in shadow. "Dammit, Gwyn, I'm tempted to shoot you myself."

He really did care. "I heard shots."

"I thought it might bring you," he said, "but I was hoping you'd be sensible."

"Seriously?"

"It could happen."

It could and often did, but it all depended on the definition of the word. "So, what do we do now?" Gwyn asked.

"*We* do nothing. You stay here. At least this way I know where you are."

Her location wasn't a great position, but she could watch his back for the most part and guard her own, as well. Plus, it gave her a decent view of the entire room. "Works for me," she said.

"If you see anything, call out." Nick slid between two pipes and disappeared into the maze of conduits. Gwyn watched and waited for either Marsha or Tucker to make a mistake so she could do some damage.

Once again, Gwyn shifted from one foot to another. Normally, she didn't mind waiting, in fact, her job required amazing amounts of patience. But taking photos of people committing insurance fraud was rarely a matter of life and death.

"I'm coming out." Marsha's words rang out in the silence. Gwyn tensed in response. What the hell was going on? Seconds later, the woman emerged on the walkway, hands over her head and walking toward Gwyn. There was no word from either Nick or Tucker, and still, Marsha advanced. Oil smudged her right cheek, and her dark hair was damp with sweat.

Despite her disheveled appearance, Gwyn didn't trust either her or her motives. "Stop right there," Gwyn called out.

Ten feet away, Marsha dropped to her knees.

Gwyn aimed her gun at the woman's chest. "What do you want?"

"He killed Stephan," Marsha sobbed. "This was just supposed to be a robbery. Just money. Not murder."

The tears didn't touch Gwyn—she remembered how cold the woman had been just an hour or so ago and ever so eager to do whatever it took to make sure she got what she wanted.

At least until she lost something. Or someone.

Then Marsha looked past Gwyn's shoulder, and her mouth curved up in a smile that made the hairs on the back of Gwyn's neck prickle to life. Tucker. Somehow, he was behind her. Seconds later, cool metal pressed against the side of her head, and the click of a gun cocking made her freeze even as she turned to verify what she knew to be true.

"Hi, Gwyn," Tucker said.

Normally Gwyn liked being right, but not this time. The heat of shame and fear washed over her. She couldn't believe she'd fallen for such an obvious ploy. If they got out of this alive, Nick would never let her live it down.

She raised her hands, holding the butt of the gun between thumb and forefinger. "How?" she asked. There was no way he could sneak past her, even in the dim lighting.

"I've worked here for the past six months," he said. "I know every door. Every hallway. And every maintenance tunnel." He took her weapon.

"And thank you," he said to Marsha. "You're a good actress."

She clamored to her feet, dusting off her wrinkled skirt. "You're welcome."

Tucker made a tsking sound. "Marsha, Marsha, Marsha. The fact of the matter is you're too good an actress."

Marsha froze, her eyes widening. "What do you mean?"

"I can't trust someone who lies that well." And before she could protest, he raised Gwyn's weapon and fired.

The shot was deafening, and Gwyn winced, but not before she saw Marsha fall back to her knees, a shocked expression on her face.

Her ears ringing, Gwyn's stomach did a slow roll. "You're a monster."

"No, I'm selfish, and I don't play well with others," Tucker said. Wrapping his arm across Gwyn's neck, he pulled her to him, forcing her to act as his shield.

"You wanted to talk?" Tucker called out, "I have your partner. Let's talk about that."

"She's not my partner." Nick's reply boomed in the dark.

Tucker shrugged. "So? You want to save her? Then I think a little sacrifice is in order."

He was going to kill Nick and let her go? Surely, Nick wasn't dumb enough to believe that. They were both dead if he gave himself up.

There was movement in the shadows. "Don't do it," Gwyn shouted.

Tucker squeezed, pressing her windpipe shut. Gwyn tried to breathe, to force any air into her lungs, but there was none. Just Tucker's grip, killing her. She pounded at his arms, but he only increased the pressure.

Nick stepped into view, arms over his head.

Out of the corner of her eyes, she saw Tucker raise her gun again. The world flickered around her, black-and-white spots that were descending into gray. A few more seconds and she'd black out, and when that happened, she'd never waken. Never see Nick. Never know if there really was a chance for a "we" between them—because neither one of them had been able to walk away. Instead, they played the hero. And sometimes, heroes died.

But not this time.

Wrenching her head sideways, her mouth found flesh, and she bit down until she tasted blood in her mouth. Tucker screamed as he fired, and his shot went wide.

Gray turned to black as the flickering behind her eyes lengthened, and in the growing dark, she saw Nick reach behind him, taking a gun from the back of his jeans.

Then world the disappeared, and Gwyn felt herself falling. She gasped.

Air.

Then hit the cement hard and fell into a heap. Was she still alive? Was Nick? With a groan, she touched her throat. It was going to be bruised as hell, but better bruised and breathing than bruised and not breathing.

Warm hands moved across her body, checking her for injury. She knew the touch. Knew the tenderness.

"Gwyn, are you okay?"

Nick. She nodded and a wave of relief washed over her. She opened her eyes. "You got him?"

"Yes," Nick said, helping her to her feet.

Just behind him Tucker lay dead on the cement.

She sighed in relief, and for a moment, she thought her knees might give. She grabbed Nick's arm until the dizziness dissipated.

"Steady there, Vampira," Nick said, putting his arm around her waist.

"I am a biter," she said, smiling.

Shaking his head, he pulled her close, his tight grip the only indication of the fear that had rocked him, as well. "You won't have a need again," he whispered. "I'll keep you safe."

He squeezed her harder. Safe. It was a warm thought.

"Back at you," she said.

Chapter 9

Gwyn wove her arm through Nick's as he walked her up the snow-covered Seattle hill and toward the women's shelter where Glory worked. Between the blackout and the fact it was three in the morning the roads were covered with snow untouched by either cars or humans.

Her sister was going to be pissed. She'd barely had time to speak to Glory before she and Nick were whisked away by the Bellevue police. After that, it was hours of giving statements and answering questions.

Glory did not do well with waiting.

"Are you sure your sister will be awake?" Nick asked, steadying her as her right foot slid on a patch of ice.

"I'm sure," Gwyn replied, regaining her balance and turning her attention to the slippery ground beneath her feet. "She won't sleep until she knows this is over and I'm okay."

"We should have called," Nick said.

"I would but I don't know her phone number. That's why I had a cell phone, so I wouldn't have to memorize things like that."

"Good point," Nick said. "But the kids will be asleep."

"And *I* won't sleep until I know they're not traumatized for the rest of their lives."

"Especially Connor," Nick said, getting to the heart of her anxiety.

She nodded. "Yes, especially Connor."

They walked in silence until they stood in front of the shelter. Gwyn held a finger to her mouth and tapped on the door.

Glory opened it, her blond hair in a ponytail, and her face devoid of makeup. "Oh my God, are you all right?" She threw her arms around Gwyn.

"I'm fine."

Behind her, the door closed with a slight squeal of old hinges.

Glory let Gwyn go then pushed past her. "And you," she poked Nick in the chest. "What were you thinking? Letting her help you? You're a cop. You should know better. I hope to hell they take disciplinary action against you for putting a citizen in danger."

Gwyn put a hand to her forehead. Just when she thought the drama was over for the night, it wasn't. Clamping a hand on Glory's shoulder, she pulled her sister away before the poke became a punch. "Back off," she said. "It's not his fault."

"Not true," Nick said.

"Damn straight," Glory said.

Gwyn shot Nick the dirtiest look she could manage. She knew he felt guilty, but giving Glory more ammunition would get her worked up, and then they'd never get her to calm down. "You are not helping."

Nick ran a hand over his dark hair, once again making the ends stand up. "But she has a point. I could have tied you up. Let the bad guys go. It's not as if there weren't options."

"And still you chose to put my sister in danger," Glory said, before Gwyn could make her own retort.

Crossing her arms over her chest, Glory fixed her anger on Gwyn. "And you. You just couldn't let him do his job, could you?"

Gwyn took a step back. Hell, she should have kept her mouth shut and let Nick take the fall. "He didn't have backup."

Glory shook her head. "Not good enough. You're always taking chances. Testing your limits. What the hell is wrong with you?"

Gwyn bit her lip and reminded herself that Glory wasn't angry. Not really. She was scared, and fear made her mean. She looked to Nick. "A little help?"

He held up his hands, palms out.

Great, he could take on a gunman but caved when it came to a pissed-off, pocket-size blonde.

"Glory." She placed a gentle hand on Glory's woven arms. "I'm sorry. I didn't mean to frighten you."

Glory didn't move. Didn't soften. "Well, you did."

"I know."

"Just promise me it won't happen again."

Gwyn wished she could. "You know I can't do that."

She might not want to be a P.I. anymore but she also knew she'd never live the safe life Glory wanted for her. The one that involved kids, a husband and no gunfire.

It wasn't in her. They both knew it.

Glory's eyes narrowed. "You always do this. You always—"

"It's Christmas Eve," Gwyn interrupted. Now was not the time, and not in front of Nick. "I just want to be happy we're all okay. Can we talk about this tomorrow?"

Glory hesitated. "Okay." Scrubbing her face, she took a deep breath. "Merry Christmas," she said, hugging Gwyn again. "I'm glad you're okay. That's the best present you could give me."

Warmth replaced the irritation, and Gwyn hugged her back. "Good. Then I can keep the necklace."

"You wish," Glory said. Letting her go, her sister gave Nick an enthusiastic hug. "Thank you for saving her life. I don't know what I'd do if she were gone."

Nick looked over Glory's shoulder at Gwyn, his expression one of confusion.

She shrugged. It took most people years to get used to her sister's mercurial mood changes. He'd deal.

Nick hugged her back. "Uh, you're welcome."

Glory let the policeman go. "The other kids are asleep, but Connor is still awake. He refused to go to sleep until he was sure you were both okay."

"Will his mother mind if we visit?" Nick asked.

"Not at all," she said, motioning them to follow.

Making sure to keep their footsteps light, they followed Glory down a hallway lit by the occasional halogen lantern. "He's in here." Glory showed them a doorway with a long curtain for a door and ushered them inside.

The room was small, furnished with two cots—one for Connor and one for his mother. The young mother was asleep, her breathing even and deep. Connor lay in bed with a flashlight, surrounded by miniature, plastic army men, his eyes shut.

Gwyn sat on the bed while Nick knelt down on the floor. Connor's eyes fluttered open and then widened when he recognized his visitors. "Hey," Gwyn whispered.

"Hey," he whispered back. His attention shot to Nick. "Santa's number one!"

Gwyn cringed at the half shout, but it seemed Connor's mother was a sound sleeper.

"Hey, buddy," Nick said, stroking Connor's blond hair. "How are you doing?"

Connor sat up. "I'm okay." He twisted his hands together. "Uh...is Santa still mad?"

Nick's brows shot upward. "What?"

"Is Santa still mad at me for running away?" Connor's eyes filled. "I was bad, but I'm sorry."

Gwyn's chest tightened. "Oh, honey, he was never mad."

But Connor waited for Nick's answer, and she couldn't blame him. After all, the policeman was Santa's number one, and you couldn't get any closer to the Big Guy.

Rising, Nick sat next to Connor. "Santa was never mad at you, Connor. You're on the Good List."

Gwyn's heart thudded harder inside her chest.

"Are you sure?" Connor asked.

"Positive," Nick replied. "I'm Santa's number one helper. Would I lie?"

"No?" he said. Gwyn didn't miss the questioning behind the small word.

Nick ruffled the top of his head. "Darned right. You are at the top of the Good List."

"And those bad guys are on the Naughty List," Gwyn said. "Forever."

Connor grinned at her, and the tension in Gwyn's chest eased. A yawn snuck out before she could cover her mouth.

"Are you going to make it?" Nick asked, one brow arched. "That was a huge yawn." He leaned in to Connor, pointing at Gwyn. "Didn't that make her look like a Pez dispenser?"

Connor giggled, and Nick smiled. "It's time for us to go, buddy."

"Do you have to leave?"

"Santa has a busy night, and he needs me at the North Pole."

Connor gave a solemn nod.

Nick lay Connor down, tucking the sheets and blankets around his shoulders. Leaning over, Gwyn kissed the top of the little boy's head then she and Nick tiptoed out, pausing to wave before they closed the curtain behind them.

"How is he?" Glory asked, leaning against the wall, waiting.

"Good," Gwyn replied.

"Think he'll be okay, or did this scar him for life?" Nick asked.

"For life? No. But they'll all get some counseling," Glory said.

"Good," Nick said. "Let me know if there is anything I can do."

Glory gave a polite nod. "I will. Thanks." She pushed away from the wall. "Now, why don't you take my sister home? It's been a long night and we all need some rest."

"How about you?" Gwyn asked, her eyes watering as she yawned again.

"I'm staying here," Glory said.

"I should stay, too," Gwyn said, torn between wanting to stay with her sister and not wanting her time with Nick to end.

Glory smiled at her—the first real smile of the night. "Thanks, but this is my place. Not yours. Go home. We'll talk later. *After* Christmas."

Gwyn knew what that conversation would entail and dreaded it, but that was a day away, and she'd take the break.

Once again, the three traversed the corridor. Glory paused at the door long enough to kiss Nick on the cheek and hug Gwyn. "Merry Christmas," she whispered as they pair stepped back into the night, and she closed the door behind them.

"She's still angry," Nick said as they walked down the hill, trying to remain upright.

"Yep," Gwyn replied, watching her feet. "But it's at me. Not you."

"Good."

She couldn't blame him for being pleased with his reprieve. Glory was petite but her temper was six foot tall. "So what next?" Gwyn asked.

"This," Nick said. "Look up."

Gwyn raised her face to the sky.

Above them, green lights rippled across the blackness and flickers of violet swirled. "Wow! The Northern Lights."

"I've heard about them but never thought we'd see them here," Nick said in hushed reverence.

She understood. Watching the lights felt like being in a church or being allowed to take part in an occasion that mere mortals weren't supposed to witness. Either way, it felt like a sign.

A confirmation that despite the day's events there was still good in the world. "It's like a miracle," Gwyn said, slipping her hand into Nick's. "A Christmas miracle."

Nick chuckled, and she lowered her gaze to meet his eyes. "You disagree?"

He shook his head. "Not at all, but I don't think that's the true miracle. Not tonight."

"Then what is?" she asked,

He tucked a strand of hair behind her ears. The warmth where his fingers touched her skin spread outward, heating her like a fleece blanket never could.

He leaned in and his mouth grazed hers in a whisper of a kiss that she felt all the way to her toes and tugged her heart.

With a sigh, Gwyn kissed him back and knew the unspoken answer to her question.

They were the miracle.

* * * * *

KISS ME ON CHRISTMAS

Jennifer Morey

To my dogs for keeping me sane as a single woman.
To my critique partners for catching all those logic errors.
Laura Leonard and Susan LeDoux, thanks for all the
reads. To Patience Smith for letting me write this story
and loving it. And to all those guys I dated who will
remain nameless—thanks for the inspiration.

Chapter 1

There that guy's date went again, with that head toss and ear-ringing laugh. She sounded like SpongeBob on pot. Shanna Toole pretended to straighten a rack of herbal teas as she covertly watched the couple sitting at a window table for two. She didn't want to be so mesmerized by them, but the weather had turned nasty and they were the only ones in her coffee shop right now.

She hoped they didn't stay long. The last news report said the airport had shut down at two. She was starting to worry about the drive home. She checked the clock on the slate-green wall behind her. Almost six. As soon as the couple left, she was going to close early.

"What do you do for a living?" Shanna heard Kane Ramsey ask. She only knew his name because he always paid with his debit card. He brought so many women into her coffee shop that she got dizzy trying to keep track. Blond. Brunette. Short hair. Long hair. Jeans. Dresses. Big boobs. Little boobs...

"I'm into real estate," the woman answered.

They came in all different professions, too. Real estate. Engineering. Business. You name it. All of them were fit and attractive. *He* was attractive. Tall. Thick, dark, blond hair that was always messy, but in a good way. Muscular, but not the Mr. Olympia type. His eyes were light green with a darker rim that accentuated them, really nice. And he had this masculine look about him. Stubble shadowed his face, and although his eyes were gorgeous, there always seemed to be a hardness about them.

"Commercial or residential?" he asked his date.

"Residential. And you're a developer? I liked your profile on Soulmate."

Shanna saw him grin. If she hadn't seen him bestow so many women that smile, she'd think it was sexy.

"I liked yours, too." He reached over and put his hand over hers, and Shanna watched the woman melt a little, like so many Soulmates before her. And he'd trolled a lot on that online dating site.

He never talked much about what he did, so it didn't surprise her that he'd maneuvered the subject away from that. He was a commercial developer who'd done several complexes in Seattle, that's really all she'd heard him say. Was he rich and didn't want the women going only for that?

She looked down from the woman's beaming face to his hand. Did he practice his timing? Maybe next time she'd clock him to see how long it took before he touched his date. Never mind that she'd imagined him touching her like that more than once.

Shanna averted her face, not feeling particularly amenable. She was going to blame her mood on her bad run of dates. And Kane, for never ceasing to remind her of them, especially the last one.

What about your family? she mouthed, keeping her head turned so the couple wouldn't see.

"What about your family?" she heard Kane ask. "Do they live around here?"

Shanna rolled her eyes. Did the man have no imagination? How could he expect to find his soul mate when he was so perfectly rehearsed? He had to be getting confused by now. After a man was with so many women, did he forget what he was look-ing for in the first place? Maybe men like him never knew, and that's why they had to bloat their calendars with so many dates.

"I'll find her somewhere, Auntie Em," Shanna mumbled under the sound of Frank Sinatra singing "Luck Be a Lady" from her overhead speakers, "even in this tornado of women."

Maybe that's why he always met them at the same place. That way he wouldn't have to remember where he told them to meet. Figures it would have to be her coffee shop. Bean Me was unique and in a great location close to the Seaside Market, but really, could he just spare her the misery of having to wit-ness his total lack of appreciation for women everywhere?

While Kane's umpteenth date rambled on about her sibling, an elderly couple came through the front door. Shanna caught another glimpse of the weather. It was getting worse. Dark now that the sun had set, but streetlights illuminated falling snow, covering thick layers of ice on poles and buildings and parked cars. Not to mention the road.

"Brrr." The old woman shivered, stomping her snow-crusted boots and keeping her pink scarf wrapped around her neck. Her husband rubbed her back as they made their way toward the counter.

"What can I get for you?" Shanna asked.

"Two large mocha skinny-dipper decafs."

Shanna turned to prepare her trademark low-calorie coffee.

"We haven't seen weather like this in years," the elderly woman marveled.

"It's really icy out there," her husband added. "There were three accidents on the walk here and we just live up the street."

"Yeah, Seattle doesn't get many of these storms." She brought the coffees to the counter and the elderly man paid.

Shanna gave him his change and caught a glimpse of Kane's thumb moving over his date's hand. It gave her an unexpected pang right in the middle of her chest. The last man she'd been with had done that. She'd met him online, and he'd wound up running her heart through a shredder.

"Thank you, dear," the elderly woman said.

"Good night," her husband added.

Shanna nodded with a smile. "Be careful out there."

They left through the front door, the husband's hand on the woman's back as they walked along the snowy sidewalk.

"Your profile said you didn't have any kids," the woman with Kane said.

Shanna pretended to be busy wiping the countertop.

"I don't," he replied.

"I have two, a seven-year-old daughter and a twelve-year-old son."

"I like kids."

"Do you want any of your own?"

Shanna subdued a smirk as Kane all but squirmed in his seat. "Er...sure, if it works out that way."

He probably had a condom in his back pocket. Wouldn't want to trap himself into anything lasting when he was still so busy trolling. Yet, how many times had she imagined him using one of them on her? Her body never listened to her brain when it came to the physical with him. He was like a forbidden fantasy she couldn't resist.

"How many times have you been married?" the woman asked.

"Once. I've been divorced for three years."

"What happened?"

"She left me for another man."

"That must have been hard on you."

Shanna stopped wiping the countertop. She could only see his profile, but she wondered why he hesitated.

"I wasn't expecting it. But maybe I should have."

"Were you faithful to her?"

"Yes."

He was probably lying. Her experience convinced her most onliners lied when it came to all the fidelity questions.

"What about you?" he asked.

"How many women have you dated on Soulmate?" she asked by return.

He paused as though he had to think. Did he want her to answer his question or had he lost track of how many women he'd seen?

"Around fifty."

The woman's eyes widened beneath her lifting brow. She was speechless for a moment. So was Shanna. That was more than even she'd have guessed. She fiddled with a stack of napkins, trying to appear inconspicuous.

"How long have you been looking?" his date asked.

"Four months."

"Four months? Boy, you've been busy!"

Shanna could vouch for that. He brought a new one in about two or three times a week. She abandoned the napkins and plucked a coffee bean from the freebie bowl by the cash register, popping it into her mouth. Good thing none of her fantasies would have a chance to come true.

The woman laughed, sounding a little unsteady. Or was that excitement? She sobered as she contemplated him. "What are you looking for?"

Was she worried or curious?

"What do you mean?" Kane asked. "In a woman or a relationship?"

"Both." The blonde leaned back in her chair, her big boobs jutting forward as she moved her shoulders back.

Shanna saw Kane notice and also didn't miss the extra seconds it took him to respond.

"I'm looking for a long-term relationship."

"Long-term?" Was the woman being cautious? Shanna sure would be. "But not marriage?"

"Depends if the relationship leads to that. And how I feel about the woman."

"What kind of woman would make you feel that way?"

"A strong one. Independent. Confident. Takes care of herself both financially and physically. I suppose I want what most men want."

"I want the same thing."

He smiled and she smiled back. Maybe they really were hitting it off. Shanna straightened a rack of gift cards, wavering between envy and pity for the woman.

That's how it had started with Mr. Inadequate. He'd smiled as if he really liked her. Touched her hand. Opened doors for her. And then that had progressed into holding hands. Kissing. Calling every day and taking her to interesting places. He even told her she was beautiful and talked about future things that included her. Then, just when she was beginning to believe they were in a real relationship, he'd dropped his bombshell.

He felt inadequate with her and he'd met someone else online. Inadequate was a new one for her. She had to hand it to him for ingenuity.

After all the men she'd gone through, all the experiences, the one she'd thought had half a chance of sticking around long enough to mean something was giving up before they'd barely started. She'd gone from feeling happy and secure, looking forward to weekend plans with a man she really liked, to being alone with an uncertain future again, struggling to understand why it was so hard for her to find a boyfriend that lasted longer than a few weeks.

Kane Ramsey was probably no different. After a few weeks, he'd get bored or scared of an impending relationship and want to find someone new. He'd keep searching for a woman who didn't exist. None were perfect enough for him, or he'd lost touch with what was.

He said something to his date and she tipped her head back with a laugh, all bleached teeth and makeup.

Would somebody just shoot her if she ever looked like that on a date? She felt embarrassed for the woman.

The lights in her coffee shop went dark. The hum of her undercounter refrigerator went silent and Frank was cut off in the middle of "Fly Me to the Moon." Shanna froze for a second, her breath hitching as she turned and looked around. It took her eyes a moment to adjust to the plunging darkness.

"What happened?" Kane's date asked.

Shanna waited for the electricity to come back on. It didn't. She could barely make out the outline of Kane and his date.

He stood from his chair and walked to the front window. His date stood, too, but stayed by the table.

"The whole street is out," he said.

Shanna joined him at the front window. Snow was accumulating on the icy road and all the parked cars. More ice hung from buildings like stalactites. A loud cracking sound penetrated the glass and then a huge tree limb crashed to the frozen road, taking out a light pole with it.

"Wow," she said. It was almost surreal.

"This isn't good," Kane said.

She shared an incredulous glance with him, catching the gleam of his amazing green eyes. Turning, she went to a display shelf and felt the items until she found the candles she had for sale there. Bringing them to the counter, she put them down. Kane went to stand near his date.

"Either of you have a light?" Shanna asked. She might have matches in the back but it would be hell trying to find them in the dark.

"I do," the woman said. She dug into her purse. Something fell to the floor and Kane bent to pick it up. A pack of cigarettes.

"You smoke?" He handed the pack to her.

"Just a little." She gave Shanna a lighter.

She took it.

"Your profile said you didn't," Kane said.

Uh-oh…

"I don't smoke all the time."

He didn't argue anymore, but Shanna wondered if it was irritation she'd heard in his tone. Was he finally getting frustrated? She lit the candles. They wouldn't put off much light, but it was better than nothing.

She hoped the electricity wouldn't be out long. She couldn't afford to lose any perishables. Especially now that the company managing her building had raised the rent. She was going to have a hard time getting by as it was.

"I'm just going to go get my radio," she said. "I'll be right back."

Lifting one of the candles, she went around the counter and into the back office. She found the small radio and pressed the power button. Nothing happened. She didn't have any batteries.

A sound up front made her abandon a futile search. She returned to the counter in time to see Gayle from the salon across the street hurry in from the blustery weather. She clutched her faux fur-trimmed jacket about her and approached the counter, eyes full of restless concern.

"I came over to see if you were all right," she said, coming to a stop at the counter. The hood of her jacket hid curly gray hair that she kept coiffed atop her head. Without coloring it, she looked every bit of her fifty-three years.

"Fine. Just waiting for the lights to come back on," Shanna said.

"They aren't going to," Gayle replied, looking taken aback that Shanna didn't know. "Not for a long time."

Shanna felt a spark of apprehension chase some of her confidence away.

Gayle must have seen it. "Haven't you heard the news?"

"Only that the airport closed."

"Power lines are going down everywhere. There are roads closing because of all the tree limbs breaking and dangerous power lines on the ground. They're advising everyone to find shelter."

Kane's date gasped and put a hand adorned with long, red fingernails to her mouth.

Gayle glanced at the woman and returned her attention to Shanna. "You should lock up and go home. Looters are bound to start roaming the streets tonight. You don't want to be here if they do."

Shanna moved her gaze to the dark window. That's all she needed. Looters.

"The weather will keep most of them indoors," Kane said,

his deep, gruff voice reassuring. "If the power is out too long the city will have patrols. National Guard will probably show up, if they aren't already on the way."

"I didn't think of that," Gayle said with an appreciative smile at Kane.

Shanna cocked her head at him, resisting the impression that he might actually be a nice guy. That was another thing she didn't need…a physical *and* intellectual attraction with him.

"I have to go home," Kane's date interrupted. She sounded anxious.

"I'll take you," Kane said, looking from her to Gayle. "I'll take you all wherever you need to go. I drive a Hummer."

Figures he'd have to brag about his Hummer.

"Don't worry about me. I'll be fine," Gayle said.

"Me, too," his date chimed in. "But it was good to meet you. Maybe you could give me a call sometime."

"What if something happens on your way? It's bad out there and you'll be alone."

"I have to go pick up my daughter."

"I can drive you."

"No, really, I'll be all right."

Shanna followed the back-and-forth conversation and wondered why the woman was so agitated.

"Then I'll follow you. Just to make sure you get home all right."

"My daughter is at a friend's, and my husband is a firefighter. I should have realized he'd be tied up—" Her eyes popped wide and her mouth O'd.

Kane stood there a moment. "Your husband?"

The woman's chest lifted and fell in the shadows of candlelight.

Shanna shared a look with Gayle, who raised her eyebrows speculatively.

"You left that out in your profile." Kane sounded injured.

"I'm sorry. I—I thought you were…you know…" She waved her hands in small circles.

"No. What?"

The woman's hands stilled and she looked up at him. "Looking for…you know…sex."

"You just wanted sex." It was a flat statement.

Shanna tried to shake herself from being so riveted.

Beside her, Gayle stifled a laugh into a nasally grunt.

Kane's date turned to look at them the same time he did. Her expression had a deer-in-headlights look, his crunched into bridled anger. But he faced his date again and held it all in check.

"I'll still take you home," he surprised Shanna by saying. She'd have thought a guy like him would just let the woman walk right out of his life so he could move on to date number fifty-one.

"No." The woman turned and went to the door, going outside and into the blustery weather. Kane followed.

Shanna looked at Gayle, who looked back. A couple of seconds later, Gayle scurried to the front door and Shanna followed, where they watched through spitting snow as Kane helped his date chisel ice off her windows while her car warmed up. The amount of ice on the windows gave Shanna's worry a nudge. It was going to be a scary ride home.

Kane finished clearing the windows and stood in the snow as the woman drove away. When the car vanished from sight, he turned and headed back toward the shop.

Gayle and Shanna stepped back as he reentered Bean Me. He stopped just inside, facing them. "We should go find somewhere else to stay. I have a room at the Warwick Hotel tonight. Maybe you should do the same. They have a generator. You could both come with me if you have nowhere else to go."

"I have a husband, one I can admit to having. And a fireplace. A real one," Gayle said, smiling. "So don't worry about me. It's her you should worry about." She swung her gaze toward Shanna and then winked her subliminal meaning Kane's way.

He looked at Shanna, unaffected. "What do you think?"

She had to stop herself from visibly flinching. "What?" He wanted her to go with him? Temptation and appall clashed inside her.

"The hotel will have power. Food."

He was only trying to be a Good Samaritan. He wasn't hitting on her. The fact that some part of her had considered it helped make up her mind.

"I have a car. And I have a dog who needs me," she said.

"All right. Where's your car? I'll help you clear the windows and make sure you make it home all right."

He seemed awfully conscientious, not wanting to leave anyone alone in the storm. Surely it was a temporary affliction. "You don't have to. Just go. I need to close up anyway."

"You should go with him," Gayle said.

Shanna sent her a silent warning.

"I'll wait for you," Kane said.

She turned back to him, unable to stop herself from looking into those dark-rimmed green eyes. She ought to know by now not to trust gazes like that—kinder than they actually were.

"Well…I better get back and close myself." Gayle started for the door, there she paused with a look over her shoulder. "You shouldn't be alone, Shanna. I came over to bring you with me, but I can see you're in capable hands." She smiled at Kane.

Shanna wanted to bop her one over the head. The woman left, her form swallowed in snow and darkness as she made her way across the street.

"Let me at least make sure you're on your way," Kane said.

Reluctantly, Shanna met his eyes again. What harm would there be in that? If she let him help her dig out her car, he'd leave and she'd be rid of him. Besides, the weather did have her spooked. And she was worried about Scotch. She could not leave her sweet little dog in a cold house, all alone and scared.

Without acknowledging him, she went to lock the front door and then returned to the counter. She opened the cash register and removed the money. Bending for a money bag, she stuffed it in and zipped it shut. With a final glance at the dark front windows, hoping no one would break them during the blackout, she blew out the candles.

Kane followed her into the back office. Tucking the bank bag into her tote, she slipped into her jacket and looped the tote over her shoulder. Outside, Shanna caught her breath against a blast of cold air.

Kane took the keys from her hand in her distraction. She decided to let him. It wasn't often she had the luxury of having someone to take care of her. He opened her car door and sat inside with one long leg still outside. Nothing happened. No headlights. No sound from the engine.

Shanna gripped her jacket tighter, snow flecking her face in the freezing breeze, making her blink. She backed up, so the building sheltered her as Kane got out and peered under the hood. After a few minutes, he slammed the hood shut and strode over to her.

"Battery's dead."

"What?" she almost shouted.

"Dead. And I don't have any cables. But don't worry. I'll take you home."

Was it really dead? She looked at her car, then him. He was an onliner. Habitual. Could she trust him?

"I'm only trying to help," he said, reading her too well.

Helpful was not a word she'd have used to describe him before the lights went out...unless it involved an orgasm. She had to remind herself not to fall for these crumbs of kindness. It was only the storm making him offer. Beyond that, some men were just good at fooling women to get what they wanted.

He put his hand on her arm and guided her toward the side of her coffee shop. Not knowing what else she could do, Shanna walked with him to the front where he'd parked his dark green Hummer H2.

There, she stopped as he opened the passenger door. She'd taken care of herself on her own for years. Did she really need this man to help her? Were his good looks making her weak? Was a secret part of her wishing a man like him would be interested in her?

No.

"I changed my mind. I don't want to go anywhere with you. I can find my own way home." She stepped back.

"Really?" He scanned the deserted, ice-caked street. "How?"

She stopped, looking one way and then the other. A single car crossed the street at a crawl a few blocks away. But then it vanished, leaving everything in darkness. Emptiness pooled in her stomach. She didn't like having to depend on him.

"Come on. You can't stay here. I'll make sure you get home. Will you be okay there?"

She turned to look at him. Would she? She wasn't even sure if she had a flashlight. She didn't have a fireplace, either. Only a few candles.

"I have a room at the Warwick. You could stay there if there aren't any others available," he said.

She opened her mouth but nothing came out. A few things crossed her mind to say, but it took her a moment to choose one. "What...you mean with you?"

"It's a suite. You can have the bedroom."

"Don't you live here?"

"I live outside of the city. When I heard the weather was going to get bad, I reserved a room for the night. Better than driving in Seattle traffic on icy roads." He looked around. "I had no idea it was going to be like this, though."

Wow. A suite with a bedroom. He must be loaded. Pieces of his conversations sprinkled into her mind. Developer.

"What do you do?" she asked.

"I'm a commercial developer." He nodded his head toward Bean Me. "This is one of my buildings."

Kane Ramsey. Of course! Why hadn't she thought of it before? He was KR Development.

"You're my landlord." She was too stunned to say anything else.

He smiled. "I thought you already knew that."

"No. I didn't know that." She stared at him while emotion coiled and churned inside her, building to anger. Then she pointed at him. "You raised my rent!"

Chapter 2

Kane took in the slender woman holding her bony wrist up and aiming a finger at him. In the darkness, her eyes looked brown, but he knew when the light hit them they turned the most intriguing shade of blue-green. The first few times he'd come to Bean Me he'd noticed her beauty and the way she laughed, so full of life and self-confidence. He'd noticed other things, too, like the way she kept interesting trinkets for sale—ornaments from all over the world and rare collectible dolls that matched the holiday season. She played a wide array of music and what little he'd heard her reveal about herself to patrons always struck him as sweet. He'd also noticed her standoffish body language. She rarely looked him right in the eye but he never missed her circumspection.

"Let's get in the truck." He opened the passenger door for her.

Folding her arms, she stuck her chin up. Snow dropped onto her creamy skin and strands of reddish-auburn hair that sprawled in layered disarray over the shoulders of her jacket.

She was probably around five-five and was fine-boned. Anything but intimidating. Yet, as little as she was, she sure packed some dynamite.

He couldn't stop a grin.

"Something's funny?"

"Get in and we'll talk."

"I don't want to go with you to your hotel room."

"Then I'll take you home, where you can freeze with your dog."

Her gaze threw darts at him in her hesitation, but finally she climbed up onto the tan leather seat and he shut the door. Walking around the front of the Hummer, he got behind the wheel and started the engine.

"Now what's this about your rent?" he asked. He'd get out and chisel all the ice off the windows in a minute.

"One of your project managers backed me into a corner."

"I'm sure he was just doing his job."

More darts flew at him from across the truck. "I argued with him for two hours but he wouldn't listen. He refused to lower his figure."

"I'm sorry, I'm not familiar with your contract. I work at a higher level than that."

"Do you pay your managers on commission? Is it your policy to hire greedy jerks?"

He'd just avoid that. Arguing would only agitate her more. "Have you already signed the contract?"

"What was I supposed to do? Not sign it and move? I have established patrons. If I moved, I'd have to start all over. Do you know how risky that would be? I've only been open a year. And now because of your company's lack of ethics, I might be driven out of business."

"I'll take a look at your contract as soon as I can."

"You should be ashamed of yourself, gouging people the way you do."

"Hey. Wait a minute. I don't gouge people. It's standard practice to raise rents yearly or when a contract is expiring. We have guidelines about that, with set percentages on increases. It's like a cost-of-living raise. Everyone needs them, including my employees, who wouldn't get pay increases if I didn't make the money in the first place."

"You could spell out the increases in your contracts. Instead of waiting until the established ones are about to expire so you can pounce."

"I'm not the one who negotiated your terms. And it doesn't sound like you did a very good job of negotiating yours."

She grunted her distain. "That wasn't negotiating. That was harassment."

"Why did you sign the contract, then?"

"I didn't have a choice!"

"You could have brought it to someone else's attention."

"Like who? *You?*"

He tried to read her face along with the way she said *you.* What did she have against him? It was more than just her rent.

Seeming to catch herself, she turned to face the window. "I'm sorry."

"Not a problem."

She looked over at him, her eyes softer now. "It's just that it came at a bad time and the increase was more excessive than I thought was appropriate."

"I'll personally look into it, I promise."

"That would be nice. If you do it." She looked straight ahead.

"Why wouldn't I?"

She just shrugged.

As the founder of KR Development, he could do something if he really wanted to, surely she knew that. He'd just told her he'd look into it. He'd even promised. Why didn't she believe him? Was it past experience with men? That had to be it. Was she so sweet that she was easily hurt? A spark of temptation struck him to find out, without hurting her. He didn't want that. But the possibility that she was as sweet as he thought started a burn inside him. He wanted to get to know her better. And despite her attempts to ward him off, he could tell she wanted the same with him.

Wait a minute. Sweet? Sweet didn't fit a busy lifestyle. He needed a tough, independent woman who had her own life and didn't need him to constantly woo her.

He climbed out of the Hummer and started scraping ice, glancing through the glass on the windshield he'd just exposed. She was watching him. Damn if the thought of wooing her didn't toy with him. He had to get a grip. He'd be setting himself up for another failure for sure if he got mixed up with this one!

If it wasn't for Scotch, Shanna would have told Kane to fend for himself. She could have gone with Gayle and slept by a nice warm fire, away from this online dating addict. She didn't like the way he'd looked at her through the windshield, wary of the hothead coffee shop girl. But also curious. She stole a glance across the truck. He drove slowly along the deserted, darkened street, both hands on the wheel, thighs slightly parted, eyes watching ahead. Relaxed as could be.

That same spark of interest that sometimes caught her off guard whenever he came into Bean Me crept into her now. And like all the other times, confusion followed. He was exactly the kind of man she was tired of meeting. What about him was different?

He slowed the Hummer even more. She looked through the snow-splattered windshield. A car that had slid off the road was just ahead. Its lights were still on. She felt the antilock brakes work as Kane stopped the Hummer beside the stranded car.

Leaving the engine running, he turned to her as he opened his door. "Wait here."

Was he being protective because he didn't want her to slip on ice? Not knowing whether to be offended or flattered, she decided to let it pass.

He approached the car and tested the driver's door. It didn't budge. He leaned close to the window, trying to peer inside through a thick layer of ice. He pounded his knuckles on the window.

Apparently no one stirred, because he moved to the rear passenger window and peered through the ice covering it. He must have noticed something, because he started yanking on the door. It must be frozen shut. He kept pulling until ice cracked and pieces fell to the ground and he opened the back door. A crying old woman bundled in a winter coat and a hat and gloves inched her way toward the edge of the seat.

Kane leaned in to help her, his strong arm going under one of hers and easily bringing her to her feet. She leaned against him, weakened from cold and fear. Her husband climbed out of the car after her, bundled like his wife, moving slow but not needing assistance from Kane.

How long would they have sat in that car?

She watched as Kane put his arm around the woman and the man gripped his other one. As they started toward Kane's truck, Shanna got out and opened the back door, her feet slipping. She used the handle to keep from falling.

She reached for the elderly man, whose breathing was as taxed as his wife's. He took her hand as Kane helped the woman into the back. She scooted over and her husband climbed in beside her.

Shanna watched them huddle close, shivering, white-skinned, lips a bluish hue. Kane stood right behind her and shut the door. Her feet slipped again but his body steadied her and he held her arm as she got back into the front seat.

A little too aware of that contact, she covertly watched him get back behind the wheel. She couldn't stop herself from observing the way his body moved as he slammed his door shut and switched the heat to high.

Then he twisted to look in the backseat. "Are you sure you're all right?"

The woman shakily nodded. "God bless you for stopping."

Kane smiled in response. "I'm Kane and this is Shanna."

"Carl and Leona Ray. It's our pleasure, I assure you." Carl

smiled back, his shivering easing with the blasting heat in the Hummer. Hugging his wife closer against him, he told Kane where they lived. It was a few blocks from Shanna's house.

"We were on our way home from the hospital," Leona said. "Our daughter just had a baby girl." Her face beamed love and Shanna envied the years of family life the couple must have enjoyed so far.

"Do you two have any kids?" Carl asked.

Startled by the question, Shanna looked at Kane the same time he looked at her.

"Uh...no," he answered.

Shanna turned toward the couple. "We aren't married."

"Oh, well, you do make an attractive couple," Leona said. "How long have you been together?"

It took Shanna a moment to reply. "We aren't."

"That's too bad. Some people just look like they belong together." The woman laughed. "How did you end up together tonight?"

Nosey old woman. "He was in my coffee shop when the power went out. My car wouldn't start so he offered to take me home."

"Ah...so maybe fate is at work after all. I didn't think I misread that. I felt the energy between you two the minute I got into this truck."

Shanna shared another look with Kane. Was there an energy between them? She felt something, but what was it? Apprehension? No. It was warmer than that. Intrigue. Attraction. Huge attraction.

As she continued to fall into his eyes, she saw them react. Her heart hammered. Thankfully, he had to glance away to drive.

"Leona's always been good at that," Carl commented. "Seeing what's going on between people."

Shanna let her breath go and looked through the passenger window at the frozen landscape.

They drove in silence for a minute or two.

"You'll both be staying at Shanna's house, then?" Leona asked, her obvious attempt to sound nonchalant failing.

"I have a room at the Warwick," Kane said. "Shanna is welcome to stay with me if her house isn't safe."

"Maybe you should do that, Shanna. It's better than being alone. And you won't have any heat in your house. Unless you have a generator."

"We have a generator," Carl said.

"I'll be fine," Shanna said.

"Don't worry, I'll make sure she stays warm." Kane sent her a sexy grin from across the Hummer.

She couldn't stop the warmth of her reaction. When he smiled like that, rational thought vanished.

Leona laughed softly. "I don't doubt that you will."

Still mesmerized by his grin, Shanna wondered what it would be like to kiss that mouth. Looking ahead at the icy road, she decided it was best just to keep quiet.

Kane pulled into a driveway and helped the older couple out.

A few minutes later he was back in the truck, and they headed toward the Beacon Hill area. He stopped to check another car on the side of the road, but that one was empty. The Hummer lights were the only lights on her street. It was eerie how dark it was. The headlights reflected on tree limbs scattered in front yards and in the street. Kane had to drive around a few.

He stopped where a bigger limb blocked the road. The tangle of power lines snaked among the debris. Shanna's heart scampered with adrenaline. Would they even make it to her house? The thought of Scotch all by herself wrenched her. The poor thing would run out of water and she'd go hungry tonight.

Kane backed the truck up to go around the downed tree. Loud cracking made him stop, the Hummer sliding a little. She twisted to see out the back window. A huge branch took out a power line and sent ice and snow flying as it blocked the Hummer's retreat with a giant crash.

Hearing her own rapid breaths, Shanna faced forward, the headlights shining on the blockage ahead of them.

She looked over at Kane, who looked back at her, just as

stunned as her. He turned to the driver's window and searched for an escape route. There was none. The tree that had fallen ahead of them lay across a yard, having narrowly missed hitting a house and now in the tangle of wire.

Kane turned the Hummer, backing to get it faced in the other direction. The tree limb that had just fallen lay across the street but it hadn't taken the lines on that side. He drove onto the curb and into someone's front yard.

Shanna caught sight of the power lines waving precariously and wondered if more would fall. Kane drove back onto the street and turned a corner. This road was better.

No sooner had Shanna relaxed against the seat, she saw someone run into the middle of the street waving their hands in the air.

Kane stopped the truck and rolled down his window.

A man approached. He wasn't very tall and wore a baseball cap over a hooded sweatshirt. He didn't seem to be keeping himself very warm.

"Man, am I glad to see you. Not many people are driving tonight. I need to get my family out of here."

"What's wrong?"

"I need your ride, man." His eyes darted from her to Kane. Something in the look made her wary.

"Maybe I can take you somewhere. Aren't you warm enough in your house?"

"A man's got to take care of his family, you know?" The short man lifted his sweatshirt and his hand came up with a gun.

Shanna gasped and sat frozen with a sudden rush of fear. What if he shot Kane? What if he shot them both?

"Get out," the short man said.

"If you need to go somewhere—"

"Get out. Now!"

Shanna's pulse charged. Kane didn't seem ruffled at all. He didn't say anything, just met the other man's desperate gaze. Then without warning, he knocked the man's gun with one hand and punched his face with his other fist. It threw the short man off balance. Kane stepped on the gas, sending the Hummer into a fishtail. Gunfire pinged against the truck. Shanna screamed and bent forward to get her head out of the way of potential bullets.

The truck seemed to be handling funny.

"He got one of the rear tires," Kane said.

"Don't stop!"

"I have to." He drove around a corner and did just that.

"Oh my God." Her mouth was dry from breathing so fast.

Kane got out and prepared to change the tire. Down the street, the shadow of a man walked toward them. When he saw that they were stopped, he started jogging toward them.

Shanna scooted to the driver's side and opened the door. "Kane!"

"I see him." He swore.

Movement from the house where they had stopped made her look there. A man with a rifle strode toward them. Did he want Kane's Hummer, too?

He cocked the rifle and aimed down the street but up in the air. When he fired a warning shot, she knew he was going to help them.

Shanna's whole body quivered from fright as she shakily looked through the back window. The man ducked for cover behind an ice-covered parked car.

The rifleman stood near Kane.

"I'll keep watch while you finish up," he said to Kane.

"Thanks. I appreciate that."

"Damn idiot's been at it for a couple of hours now. Trying to steal a car. Called the cops but it'll be a while before they can do anything. Whole city's gone mad."

"Thank you for helping us," Shanna said.

"You folks need a place to stay? Got me a generator and the wife is making a big pot roast. Got a few of the neighbors here, but we can make room for more.

"We'll be all right," Kane said from where he worked on the tire, and Shanna trusted him.

He finished with the tire and stood. Snow flecked his shoulders and hair. He shook the rifleman's hand and thanked him before getting behind the wheel.

Shanna checked once more to see where the man who'd tried to steal the Hummer had gone, but saw nothing. She leaned back against the seat and watched as Kane meandered around debris in the road. It took several minutes to get just a few blocks, but finally they reached her street.

Pulling in front of her two-story house, Kane left the truck running. The headlights from the Hummer helped her see. When he got out with her and followed her to her front door, she stopped digging for her keys to look at him. He was going with her?

"Just in case you have company you weren't expecting," he answered her silent question.

She resumed her dig for keys and found them, then climbed the steps to her covered porch and opened the door. The living room was dark and cold.

"Scotch," she called. When she didn't hear her cocker spaniel's claws tapping on the hard wood floor, she felt a flash of worry.

She walked straight ahead into the dining and kitchen area. No Scotch. Back in the living room, she passed Kane and jogged upstairs, hearing him follow at a slower pace.

On the second story, she flipped the light switch and remembered there was no power. The hall was pitch-black.

"Scotch," she called again, walking down the hall, she paused at her guest room. Peering inside, she felt a breeze and heard rustling. Through the shadows, she made out the shape of a tree limb sticking through the window. Her heart sank. But there was nothing she could do about it.

"Could be worse," Kane said from behind her.

Ignoring him, she closed the door and moved around him on her way down the hall. At the end, she went into her master bedroom. Her eyes were better adjusted to the darkness. She heard something and caught the shadow of movement on the bed.

She let her breath go. "Scotch." Relief washed over her. She went to the bed and knelt before the cocker spaniel, hearing and feeling her warm, excited breaths, and then a little whimper.

"Good girl." She kissed the dog's furry cheek, feeling equally furry eyebrows move with blinks. It must have frightened her when the tree limb had fallen, otherwise she would have barked when Shanna came home.

"Poor baby." She faced Kane. "I should grab a few things."

He stood in the doorway, a looming shadow. Was he going to watch her pack?

"I'll wait for you downstairs."

How had he guessed her thoughts? She hadn't even had to say anything. He was probably good at reading every woman...with all the practice he'd had.

She groped in the dark for her overnight bag and threw in a change of clothes and some toiletries. Scotch stayed close to her feet.

"I won't let any more nasty tree limbs scare you," she said. Closing the bag, she headed downstairs.

Kane stood by the front door, watching her as she descended, at least she was pretty sure he was through the darkness. For a second she considered telling him she and Scotch would tough out the night in the cold and dark. But not only did that idea not appeal to her, there was the matter of the tree sticking into her guest room. And that man who'd shot at them. She could stay with Carl and Leona, but their house was too close to that trouble. Maybe she could take shelter with her friend Tiffani. She'd call and find out.

"I need to get some dog food." She went into the kitchen and put a small baggie of food in her overnight bag along with a bowl for water. Then she found Scotch's leash and clipped it to her collar. Scotch licked her cheek, making Shanna smile.

Back in the living room, Kane took her bag and she grabbed her purse and led Scotch out the door. In the Hummer, she found her cell phone. Scotch jumped from the backseat and stepped onto her lap. Shanna put her arm around her and gave her a peck of a kiss on the top of her head.

Beside her, Kane looked down at the dog and then at her. She doubted he had any dogs of his own. He was probably too busy being a corporate shark.

Lifting her cell phone to her ear, she listened to ringing until Tiffani's voice mail sounded. Dammit. She called information and then the Hilton. They didn't have any rooms left. It was the same for the Westin and the Sheraton. Apparently a lot of people had the same idea. Go stay in a hotel, where there were backup generators. She dropped the phone into her purse and pet Scotch.

"There are worse things than being stuck with me," Kane said.

Seeing his smiling profile, she wondered. If he kept attracting her like this, she'd end up swimming with the other fifty fish.

"Is it just me you don't like or men in general?" he asked.

Though he sounded teasing, she sensed he really wanted to know. "It's not that I don't like you, I've just seen how you operate. I lost count around the twelfth date, but you must have brought about thirty women into my coffee shop. What do you expect me to think?"

"That bothers you?" he asked with a glance.

Yes. "Of course not."

"What's wrong with dating a lot of women?"

"Nothing." It made him seem indecisive and untrustworthy.

"It's not like I slept with all of them."

But he had slept with some of them.

"I didn't sleep with most of them."

That made her lift an eyebrow. Did he know what she was thinking?

He caught her gaze. "I only slept with one."

Okay, that was impressive. She faced forward, uncomfortable with the way that satisfied her.

The sound of his chuckle warmed her. "I'm going to be a gentleman, here, and not ask you the same question."

"You want to know how many men I slept with?"

"No."

Yes. She smiled. "One. Just like you. How long has it been for you?"

"Six months."

"Three for me."

This was starting to resemble the question-and-answer phase of a really good date. Covering a lot of ground, here....

"What happened?"

"He didn't think he was enough for me."

She watched him think about that a moment. "I can see how a guy would do that."

"You can?"

"You're a smart, successful woman. I'd run, too, if I couldn't satisfy you."

She felt her face begin to heat. "What happened with your relationship?"

"She got tired of my work schedule."

"You know, you're really going to have to address that."

"I just haven't met the right woman yet."

"Slow down a little and you will." He was way too much of a workaholic.

"Are you always this open with men?"

"Yes."

He shook his head with a brief but amused laugh. "I should have gone with my gut and asked you out."

"What?" He'd wanted to ask her out? She struggled to keep the pleasurable response circulating through her core from showing on her face or in her body language. She'd learned to get practiced at that, but this time seemed different. He seemed to push her limits on a fundamental level.

"I didn't think you were interested."

"I'm not. I wasn't." Dang it. She'd said that too quick!

He eyed her dubiously, amusement still crinkling his eyes.

"Okay, I can see it's time to stop this conversation." And fast.

"Are you scared?" he teased.

"No."

"Would you have gone out with me?"

"No!"

He looked over at her. "Would you go out with me now?"

She could only stare at him. Go out with him. Mr. Onliner.
"Uh…" Yes!

"Just forget I said anything."

Fat chance of that happening. Shanna marveled at his disappointed profile and began to worry she was falling for the wrong guy…yet again.

Chapter 3

Kane followed Shanna and her dog to the elevator. After convincing her the Warwick didn't have any rooms left, she'd finally agreed to come up to his room. He had to admit, this was unusual, but the circumstances were unusual. He didn't want her to spend the night cold and alone. He wouldn't want anyone to have to do that. It wasn't her nice butt that motivated him. Or the chemistry that had pleasantly surprised him on the way here.

Opening the door to his suite, he let her in ahead of him. She looked around the spacious living room, a soft green and yellow sofa sat before an armoire. Near the floor-to-ceiling windows, a small table for two offered a great view of downtown. Through a door to the left was the master bedroom and bathroom with a jetted tub.

He put her bag in the master bedroom and came back into the living room. She'd unleashed her dog and it sat next to her, both of them staring at him.

The silence grew deafening.

"You want to go grab something to eat?" he asked. It was too uncomfortable up here, just the two of them. The dog didn't count.

She nodded. "That would be great."

"Will...ah...Scotch be ok in here alone?"

"Oh, yeah, she's a good girl."

"Why'd you name her Scotch, anyway?" he asked as they left the room.

"Because I was drinking it when my friend brought her to my house and she was the same color."

"Do you drink a lot of scotch?"

"Only that one time. I think that was after Bachelor Number Thirteen."

"Having about as much luck as I am, huh?"

She didn't respond to that, but he could tell it was a sore subject.

He stopped himself from putting his hand on her lower back as they stepped onto the elevator. She wasn't his date. Maybe he had gone on too many of those lately. He just didn't believe in wasting time, and he wanted to find a girlfriend who'd hopefully grow into more so he could straighten out that part of his life. He didn't want to be alone anymore.

On the main level, the halls and lobby were dimly lit, the hotel conserving energy by only using half its lights. None of the exterior lights were on. The sound of a crowd of people carried into the open space. The Brasserie Margaux was busy. No surprise. He bet every place in the city that had hot food and a generator was busy tonight.

He stopped before the hostess.

"It'll be an hour wait," she told him. "We're out of chicken and lamb on our dinner menu and tiger prawns on our tapas menu."

"Thanks. We'll take our chances in the bar." He led Shanna there. A throng of people stood and sat at the bar and at tables, laughing and talking. Above the bar, a television played a news program on CNN. He found a place to stand at the edge of the bar area and watched a video segment display varying clips of a dark Seattle. The extent of the outage was staggering. Sections of the city had lost power one at a time since early afternoon.

"Oh my God," Shanna exclaimed beside him.

More footage showed downed power lines laden with ice. There were so many.

"It's going to take days to get the power back on," Shanna added.

Yeah, and that's what worried him. He glanced around the throng. Did the hotel have enough provisions to support this many people? He didn't have any food in his suite, other than snacks the hotel stocked. He hadn't thought they'd need to stay more than one night.

"Good thing I don't have any plans for Christmas," he said.

"I was going to drive to Portland tomorrow."

Even if she could make it out of the city in this weather, she had no car. The rental companies would probably not be open, either, without power to operate.

"Looks like you're going to be stuck with me for a little longer than you thought."

Her head turned from the television and she stared at him, a blank look, as if she were struggling to comprehend spending Christmas with him.

"Don't worry, I won't take it personally," he said.

The blank look remained and he couldn't help smiling.

"Would you like something to drink?" he asked.

"Uh…sure. Water."

He turned.

"Wait."

Stopping, he looked back at her.

"Make that a dirty martini. Tanqueray."

"Is this another Scotch moment?"

She smiled. "Nope."

Smiling back, he made his way through the crowd to the bar and five minutes later returned with a martini and a beer and two bottles of water tucked under his arm. He handed her the martini.

She lifted the drink and sipped. Her eyes were that blue-green color again. She had a slender nose and plump lips and prominent cheekbones. Her hair was uncombed but it looked good that way, with all its layers. She had a lot of it, too. Enough to sink his fingers into and pull her head back for a long kiss.

Whoa. Where had that come from? He drank some beer and pretended to study all the people around them. But his interest soon gravitated back to Shanna. She was wearing jeans and high heels that made her seem taller than she was. Her tan sweater molded to her nice breasts. Not too big, not too small.

There he went again. Noticing her that way. Dating her was one thing, but this animal attraction had flared so fast he could hardly keep up with it.

He drank some more beer. Was he mistaking the answering warmth? She'd never shown any hints of it at the coffee shop. But now...

The hostess called a name and the couple sitting at the table beside them got up. Shanna climbed onto one of the seats. He put the waters on the table and sat across from her. A woman came and wiped the table and took the dirty glasses away. He sipped his beer and put it on the table.

Funny, how the city was shut down and they had their own little oasis. What a stroke of luck that he could enjoy dinner with a beautiful woman while chaos took place outside the hotel walls. He looked over at Shanna.

"Well, I already know what you do for a living...what about your family? Do they live in Portland?"

She looked at him as though she couldn't believe he'd asked. "I'm not one of your dates, so don't start following your script."

He leaned back in his chair, a little stunned. "What script?"

"You ask all your dates that question."

"Were you listening that closely?"

She averted her gaze, scanning the crowd without appearing to pay much attention to what she saw.

"How else was I supposed to get to know them?" he pressed.

Turning back to him, she contemplated him. Frustration beamed off her. But then slowly her temperament smoothed, as if she realized she'd revealed too much emotion.

That interested him. She didn't want to get to know him, or she wasn't going to let herself. Either he'd have to work hard to get her to open up, or give up now and just get through the blackout.

He sipped his beer and watched two couples laughing at a table near theirs.

"My parents and my brother and his wife and three kids live in Portland," she said.

He smiled as he looked at her again. Was she just being civil or was temptation playing a role, too? "I have a brother in San Diego. My parents and sister and older brother live in Broken Bow, Nebraska."

"And you weren't going to see them for Christmas?"

"I've been busy with work. A new acquisition, and some re-organization going on."

"You're working over Christmas?"

He shrugged. "It happens sometimes."

"And you were married once?"

"Now who's following a script?" he teased.

She smiled and gave her head a little shake. "Sorry. I guess I'm a little tainted right now."

"That bad, huh?" Must have been hurt by a man. "How long were you with him?"

"You didn't answer my question."

"You already know the answer."

She knew a lot about him, what with her eavesdropping and all. It should bother him, but it didn't. Instead, it flattered him to know she was so curious.

"We didn't date that long," she said. "He was just another online player, claiming to be looking for something long-term, when in fact, he was dating anything that responded to his e-mails."

"Not everyone is like that on those sites."

Her eyes changed to mocking skepticism.

"I may have dated a lot of women, but I also know what I'm looking for."

"And after fifty attempts you haven't found it?"

He couldn't deny it looked bad. Was he being too picky? "Most of them were one-time dates. A few of them had potential, but either they lost interest or I did. The one that came close decided she didn't want to be with an executive. It's nothing immoral."

"You spend holidays alone to work and you aggressively pursue women. What are you looking for?"

"You mean, you didn't hear that when you eavesdropped on my conversations?"

She lowered her eyes and turned her martini glass in a circle. She had heard. He found that incredibly tantalizing.

"Were you ever married?" he asked.

"No, but I was engaged once. I was with him for ten years, but I finally realized he wasn't right for me. We were too different, and we were growing apart."

"How many men have you dated since then?"

She sipped her martini and didn't respond. He grinned because he could tell she knew what he was after. She didn't even have to answer. She'd dated a lot of men.

"I wasn't looking for meaningless sex," she protested.

"Neither am I."

"Okay…then maybe you're just looking for someone who will neatly fit into your busy schedule. Someone who won't complain about the hours you work."

Her observation was accurate. But why did it sting coming from her? "What's wrong with that? I want someone who accepts me the way I am."

"Maybe that's why you're having such a hard time finding her. What woman wants a man who's only willing to offer mediocre to a relationship?"

"I'm not offering mediocre."

"No?"

"Do you always say exactly what's on your mind?"

She breathed a laugh and he could tell she'd realized she might be getting a little too harsh. "I'm sorry. It's just, if it was me dating you, I wouldn't want to come second to your company."

"If I was dating you, I doubt that would be possible."

Her smile remained and she took her time replying. "Do you say that to all the girls?"

"No." Amazing. He hadn't.

Reluctance to believe him hovered in her beautiful blue-green eyes.

"What are you looking for in a man?" he asked, not wanting this conversation to end. He wanted to get to know her, more than he'd wanted to get to know any other woman before her. "You probably want the usual. Fidelity, honesty, all that, but what about the man? What do you want from him as a person?"

He watched her genuinely ponder his question. "I...I guess I just want someone who fits. Someone who understands the way I think and likes it. Someone who makes me laugh and who I can be myself with and am physically attracted to."

"And you've never found it? Not even with one or two?"

A frown put a crease between her eyebrows. "I thought I found it with the last guy, but he dropped a bomb on me when he broke it off. I wasn't expecting it. I thought we were hitting it off, and all along he was thinking the opposite."

"Dating can be that way."

"Yeah. I sure am sick of it." She smiled wryly.

He returned the smile. "I am, too."

"A real connection is always missing," she said. "Sometimes I get close, but it never quite fills the bucket, you know?"

"Yeah, I do." Boy did he ever. The similarities between them were beginning to resonate a little too much. Why had they both dated so many people and not found what they were looking for? And why were they connecting like this? Why her? Why now?

She didn't say anything more, so he sipped his beer and

glanced around the bar. He spotted someone that made him stop. His date from the coffee shop. She sat at the bar, drink in front of her, alone, and looking at him with a sullen pout. She must not have made it home from the coffee shop. He wondered how she'd gotten to the hotel. Had she slid off the road and gotten a ride or had road closures turned her around?

"I hope her daughter is okay," Shanna said, turning from looking over her shoulder.

He couldn't help the flash of irritation. "I'm sure her *husband* took care if it."

The tiny smile said she was stifling a full grin. It worked to defuse his wavering mood.

"I thought someone like you wouldn't mind meeting a woman who was only after sex. It's sort of a refreshing change, isn't it? The woman after it instead of the man, I mean."

Someone like him? "If I wanted a married woman, I'd have never gotten divorced."

"Why did you get divorced, anyway?"

"Are we on a date now?"

"No."

She seemed indignant enough to amuse him. "Yes, we are. And you already know the answer anyway."

"She left you for another man. I know. But why'd she go looking?"

"She didn't support my choice in careers."

"In other words, you didn't pay enough attention to her."

"I was with her every spare moment I had." But somewhere inside him he knew she was right.

"When? The few minutes before you fell asleep every night? And then there must have been the times you traveled."

"I asked her to go with me a lot of the times."

"If you really wanted your marriage to work, you would have found time to be with your wife. I think you just wanted the convenience."

"Convenience?"

"I've met so many men like you. You've invested so much

of yourself in your career that you don't know what you want for anything else in your life. It's a miracle if you can decide with any certainty what kind of music you like, much less what you want a woman to have between her ears. It's the stuff between her legs that counts most."

Ok, that was going too far. "Hey, I wasn't the one who burned you."

She sank back against the chair, repentance in her eyes. "He didn't burn me. I didn't care enough for him to have that much of an affect on me. He just showed me what a fool I've been, searching online for someone worthy enough to take seriously."

"Not every man who uses online dating sites is bad."

"Are you trying to tell me you're one of those men?"

"Yes."

"I've heard that before."

"You didn't meet me online."

She didn't have anything to say to that, but her eyes still held a sarcastic distrust that he found endearing.

He smiled and flagged the waitress for the bill. At least he wasn't going to be bored while the city was paralyzed under ice.

The restaurant ran out of eggs and sausage by ten the next morning, so Shanna had called for oatmeal. Now it was after one in the afternoon and Kane wasn't back from wherever it was he'd gone. When she'd awakened, he wasn't there. She should be glad for the reprieve. Spending so much time with him was beginning to wear on her. Could she afford to trust him? He'd dated fifty women. What made her any different than all of them? It would be sweet to believe she was, but reality wouldn't be so kind. If she got involved with him, would she just be signing herself up for another heartache?

She paced by the television. "The airport has reopened, but most of Seattle remains without power today and there's no indication of when it will be restored…" a news anchorwoman said.

How long was she going to be stuck here? Tomorrow was Christmas. She'd already called her mother on her cell. She hadn't had service until late this morning.

What if she woke up on Christmas morning with Kane?

She stopped pacing. She wanted to.

Worse, she missed him right now. She didn't know where he was and that bothered her—like they were a couple. It had only been a day and she was already attached. What was the matter with her?

She had to do something.

Grabbing her jacket and purse, she checked on Scotch curled up on the couch and then left the suite. On the main level, she passed the lobby with its dark wood and copper fireplace. People sat around it, some talking, some reading. She didn't see Kane's long-lost date. She reached the front doors.

"Excuse me, Ms.?" someone called from her right.

Shanna stopped and looked at a man dressed in a hotel security uniform, standing next to the entrance.

"The National Guard is patrolling the streets. If you don't have to go anywhere, I'd suggest you didn't."

"I have a coffee shop not far from here. I want to make sure it hasn't been looted. I can walk there."

"National Guard has everything under control in the downtown area. You don't need to worry."

Well, that was good news, anyway. She wasn't so sure about not worrying, though. But even if her shop had been looted, the National Guard was in the area. What more could she do?

"Thank you." She turned and headed for the restaurant, where it appeared everyone else had gathered. Like last night, it was crowded. She entered the throng, listening to the chatter, hearing a few slurring words. Some had decided to spend their time drinking. She found a small table and sat. A day-old newspaper lay there, so she started reading.

But it wasn't long before her thoughts turned back to Kane. The prospect of getting involved with him scared her. Maybe she should shut him out until she was able to go home.

And then what? Never try love again? Is that where she was headed?

Maybe all those dates just hadn't been right. Maybe the men had all been wrong for her. Did she want to pass up the chance that Kane could be different?

She wasn't sure she could risk it. Kane liked women too much. Or was that really what drove him? Maybe he was searching just as hard as she was? Maybe they were looking for the same thing. Except he was looking for the wrong thing. He wanted a woman who fit his schedule, when what he needed was a woman who fit *him*.

Kane left his office and made his way back toward the Warwick. The weather had cleared but it was still cold. Ice clung to eaves and light poles and cars, but signs of a meltdown were beginning. Cleanup efforts were heavily under way. The main roads in the downtown area were being cleared. Workers were busy repairing power lines.

After two hours trying to work, he finally admitted the real reason he'd left the hotel room. He hadn't wanted to be there when Shanna woke. Seeing her again, in the morning, in his hotel room, would have driven him mad. He wanted her. All morning he'd tried to tell himself it was just physical. She was an attractive woman. What man wouldn't have sexual fantasies of going into her room and stripping her naked? He'd barely slept because of those tortuous thoughts.

He came upon Hisashi's Bar and Grille and spotted Hisashi hammering plywood over his broken windows. Kane veered across the street.

Hisashi saw him and stopped hammering, climbing down from his stepladder.

"Mr. Ramsey, what are you doing out at such a time? Did you not make it home yesterday?"

"What happened?" he asked instead of answering.

Hisashi shook his head as an expression of angst and anxiety consumed his face. "Last night a group of young boys broke into my restaurant. They take everything from my register. A whole day's worth. It will not be easy to recover this, what with all the repairs I must now do."

An impulse hit him. It was Christmas Eve and he was going to spend it with Shanna. She didn't trust his intentions, but if he showed her he wasn't like her other dates, maybe he could make this thing between them last long enough to see where it led.

"You have any fresh seafood in there?" he asked Hisashi.

"Ya, ya. I had a small generator. At least I have not lost that."

"Good. I'd like to order takeout." He pulled out his wallet and counted a thousand dollars. "Will this help?"

Hisashi shook his head and waved one of his hands. "No, no. You no need to do that."

"Take it. Make me a nice dinner for two."

Hisashi smiled big and took the money. A half hour later, Kane had a bag of fresh food. And wasn't Shanna going to be surprised?

Would she think he was trying to seduce her? Let her. Because he was. And a lot more than that. He wanted to explore her. She was the first woman he'd met in a long time who stimulated him on a deep level. Challenged his thinking, his ideals.

Entering the hotel, he rode the elevators to their floor and opened the door to his suite. Shanna wasn't in the living room. It was getting late.

She wasn't in the bedroom, either, but seeing the unmade bed reminded him of the thoughts that had plagued him all night. That's when he could no longer deny it. Along with his fantasies, the things she had said last night, made him confront, had run through his head, too.

He'd divorced a woman who hadn't been able to handle his work schedule and he was in danger of repeating the mistake. He'd told himself he wanted a woman who could handle his ambition, but the truth had reared up in his conversation with Shanna. How had she managed to do that?

She wasn't afraid to say what was on her mind, for one.

Maybe she felt as if she had nothing to lose. She saw him as a man she'd never end up with, so why not? It had opened his eyes.

Did he really want a woman who fit his work first and everything else second? Someone who'd stay in the background while he conquered the corporate world? His ex had accused him of never wanting to spend time with her. Now he knew she'd been right. He didn't want that again. He wanted to be consumed with a woman. And he wanted to see if that woman could be Shanna.

Chapter 4

"I wondered where you were."

Shanna looked up from the newspaper and saw Kane standing there. Feeling a rush of pleasure with the sight of him, tall and gorgeous with a voice to match, she stiffened. It was after four. She hadn't seen him all day.

His shoulders were broad in a light blue jean shirt, and his dark blue jeans fit him good, no stomach pushing the waistband too low. And she could see the outline of his package. A man who looked this good in jeans had to be worth something.

"I went up to the room. I thought you left," he said.

"Did you miss me?" she teased.

He grinned. "Yes."

A funny flutter down low and deep caught her off guard. Was he flirting with her? She stopped smiling when she realized she'd flirted first.

As he moved to the other side of the table, she got a glimpse of his fine ass. He sat across from her.

"Where'd you go?" she asked.

"To the office. It's within walking distance."

He'd gone to work on Christmas Eve, when the city was without electricity. "Just couldn't resist, huh?"

"I didn't get much done."

"Kind of hard in the dark."

The slight cock of his head and look of umbrage made her wonder if work was the only reason he'd gone.

"That was part of the distraction," he said.

"There were others?" She was afraid she didn't sound casual enough.

"Plenty." Leaning back against his chair, he watched her the way a man does when he likes a woman a lot. That captivated look in his eyes.

She couldn't help smiling. "Care to share any of them?"

"I better not."

"That good, huh?"

"You have no idea."

That almost made her ask him to tell her.

"That's the real reason I left this morning."

"Wow." He was either really good at getting into a girl's panties or just plain charming.

"Yeah."

"Am I safe tonight?" Putting her elbows on the table, she folded her hands and put her chin on top, feeling like a flirty fifteen-year-old.

"As safe as you want to be."

She laughed lightly. It was too good not to, especially when those green eyes took in her face as if she were a sculpture of a naked woman.

"Do you trust me?" he asked.

Yes. Almost. "No." She wanted to.

"Fair enough. I picked up a few things on my way back here. How about you consider tonight our first date?"

"What did you pick up?"

"You'll see. Later." The left side of his mouth lifted and his eyes sent her a sexy message.

Oh, that tickled her insides. "Why can't you tell me? Is it kinky?"

"Do you like kinky?"

"I have my boundaries." She couldn't believe she was playing along with this. And liking it.

"I'll keep that in mind."

Lifting her chin off her hands, she leaned back and just looked at him. His gaze flared like a windswept grass fire. She should be running from it. Instead, all she wanted to do was feel it envelop her.

Arguing from the entrance of the bar made her turn with Kane. A woman stood before a tall man with dark hair. He spoke angrily to her, but not loud enough for Shanna to discern what was being said over the other people in the bar. Though she could only see the woman's back, she recognized her.

"Isn't that your date from yesterday?" she asked, incredulous.

"Yeah." He didn't sound happy.

The man searched the bar.

"Must be the husband." Was he looking for his wife's date? "Does he know about you?"

Shanna watched the man spot Kane and start toward them.

"Looks like it."

"Oh, boy," Shanna said, getting worried. She didn't want to be in the middle of a bar fight over a married date that Kane met online.

The woman marched after her husband, trying to take hold of his arm as he reached Shanna and Kane's table.

Kane stood as the man came to a halt.

"What the hell are you doing here?" the man demanded.

Shanna watched Kane remain silent, as if allowing the man to answer his own question. City-wide blackout.

"I'm not stupid, mister. I know who you are. You're the guy my wife's been seeing. I recognize you from that online dating site."

"Todd, stop this. I didn't come here to see Kane," Kane's date said.

"Kane?" The angry husband could have drilled holes through his wife's eyeballs with his look. "You say his name like you've said it many times."

"I haven't, I—"

"I always knew you were a tramp."

The woman sucked in a breath of air. "That isn't fair."

The volume of voices lowered around them. Some of the people in the bar were beginning to notice the ruckus.

"Look," Kane said, "I didn't know your wife was here. She must have gotten her own room."

"I did," the woman said, tugging on her husband's arm. "Come on, let's go. Don't make a scene, Todd. We can talk about this in my room."

"You e-mailed him. I read them all."

"Only to arrange a time and place to meet. We only met once."

"You're lying. And there was more in those e-mails than arranging a time and place to meet. You like him."

"I only met her once," Kane said. "But I wouldn't have even done that if she'd have told me she was married." He pinned the woman with a hard glare of disgust.

"I think you've been sneaking around with my wife," the man said.

"I didn't know she was married," Kane repeated. "She didn't tell me, and she lied in her profile. I would have never pursued her otherwise."

Todd swung his gaze to Kane's date.

"Todd, please. Stop this. Let's go to my room," she pleaded.

It was like a bad movie Shanna couldn't stop watching. She was one of the background actresses, a prop, not noticeable enough to pay any attention to. Not that she wanted to be noticed right now. She'd like nothing more than to go to the room and snuggle with Scotch.

"Don't you mean the same room you planned to bring *him?*" the husband shouted, the epitome of a man victimized by his ego.

The woman looked at Kane with big, round, revealing eyes. She *had* meant to bring Kane here.

"Oh my God," her husband said, an appalled frown on his mouth and in his eyes.

"What did you expect?" the woman spat. "We haven't had sex in weeks!"

"You slept with him?"

"No."

The husband turned to Kane. "Unscrupulous swine!" He swung his fist. Kane didn't move in time and was struck on his cheek.

He tried to catch his balance, but tripped over the foot of a man standing behind him and fell on his rear.

Shanna sprang to her feet and planted her palms on the husband's chest, shoving as hard as she could. The man stumbled but didn't move far. He turned his injured ego onto her.

"Bitch."

Her jaw opened and she almost let her temper loose. But she caught the knee-jerk reaction in time.

Kane climbed to his feet. "I think you should both go." He was bigger and taller than the other man. Had he been prepared for the punch, his date's husband wouldn't have stood a chance.

From the bar entrance, two security guards approached.

The husband saw them and faced Kane again. "This isn't over. I'm not finished with you."

Kane didn't react. Just waited for the security guards to stop before them.

"Let's go," Kane's date said, tugging her husband's arm.

He relented, raising his hand to the security guards. "We're going." And then to Kane, "Don't come near my wife again."

"He didn't know, Todd. I went on Soulmate to find someone to have sex with, that's all."

"That's all?"

"Come on, let's go to my room." She tugged on his arm again.

He didn't budge. "I don't want to go anywhere with you. Did

you know I was going out of my mind worrying about you? When the airport closed, I couldn't reach you."

"I'm sorry."

"And then you didn't pick up our daughter. I had to leave work to go and get her."

"Were is she? Where is our son?"

"They're at my sister's. Where I'm going." He turned and started off.

"Wait!" She held on to his arm, trying to stop him. "What if you don't make it?"

He shrugged her off him. "What do you care?"

"I do care."

At the bar entrance, he stopped and faced her and they argued at a low volume. Finally his temper eased and they left together.

The volume of talking gradually increased in the bar. Distinguishable words meshed together as the throng conversed among pairs and groups.

Shanna turned to Kane, who rubbed his cheek. "Are you okay?"

"He's lucky I didn't see that coming."

"Ok, Batman. You ready to go up to the room?"

He dropped his hand and smiled. "Yes."

As it dawned on her how her question sounded, she pivoted and walked toward the elevators.

In the suite, Shanna held Scotch while she watched Kane go over to the bar. Putting Scotch down on the couch, she joined him there.

"Would you like a drink?" he asked.

"Sure. Whatever you're having."

He poured martinis into two glasses and handed her one. Their gazes met and she couldn't look away.

"I'm starting to see why you don't like the online thing."

She smiled and reached up to hold his chin with her fingers and thumb, turning his head aside so she could better see the reddened skin of his cheek. No blood.

"He can't hit worth a darn."

Kane chuckled and she lowered her hand, taking a sip of her martini.

"You never answered my question."

"What question was that?"

"Are you going to consider tonight our first date?"

"That depends."

"On what?"

"On what you have planned."

He grinned. "All those times I came into Bean Me, I wondered what it'd be like if it was you sitting across from me."

"You did not." Did he? She'd seen firsthand what kind of ladies' man he was. While he was charm incarnate, she still didn't trust his intentions.

"You never seemed interested."

"You were with other women." A lot of them. He was too hard to please. She'd be an idiot to fall for him. But maybe she had one more risk left.

"There is that."

"What would you have done if I'd have shown interest?"

"Probably come in by myself." He sipped his drink while his gaze took a leisurely trip down her chest and returned to her eyes.

"And then what? Ask me out on a date?"

"Probably."

Just probably? "And then what?"

"Ask you out on a second date."

"You don't know that. You've never gone out with me."

"I've been with you for more than twenty-four hours. I'd have asked you."

He sure knew how to feed her ego. But he was right. Instead of getting sick of each other, they seemed to keep getting closer.

She sipped her drink and let herself feel the pleasure it gave her to look into his incredible eyes. The energy between them hummed.

"What made you decide to open a coffee shop?" he asked, and she was relieved to move on to another topic.

He sipped his martini and she was distracted watching his lips.

"I was an engineer at Boeing. I got tired of the corporate environment."

"What'd you do for Boeing?"

"I was a test engineer. I did a lot of requirements and specifications and ran tests on aerospace products, that kind of thing."

"Sounds like you gave up a good job."

"I wasn't happy. I wanted to work for myself, so I used my 401K to get Bean Me going." Reminded of her rent situation, she lowered her eyes and sipped her drink. She'd been doing fine until her rent was raised. It wouldn't happen overnight, but unless business picked up or she raised her prices, she'd gradually go under. There were plenty of other coffee shops, and if she raised her prices, she'd price herself right out of the market.

"Are you hungry?" he asked.

Looking up, she met his smiling eyes. "So it's dinner you have planned."

"For our date. When are you going to admit that's what's happening here?"

"All right. It's a date. But don't get any fresh ideas."

With a cagey grin, he moved around her and bent to open the refrigerator.

What was she getting herself into?

He brought out a container of sushi.

Shanna's stomach growled. "How did you get that?"

"From a restaurant I frequent. I know the owner." Putting the container down on the counter, he opened a smaller one of soy sauce.

"Must be nice to have people do what you want all the time." She picked up a salmon roll and dipped it in the sauce.

"He's a friend of mine."

She chewed the roll. "Mmm."

He ate one, too, watching her mouth as she chewed another one. She looked at his mouth, too. There went that energy again. She met his green eyes and once again let herself feel the attraction mixing.

"What's the main course?" she asked, getting a little breathless.

"Tempura. Cold, but good."

"I don't think I've ever had Japanese on Christmas Eve before." And she had to say, it wasn't disappointing. She hadn't expected much with the city powerless and the hotel running low on food. She glanced around the fancy suite. "All that's missing is a Christmas tree."

He gestured with the nod of his head toward the wall across from the floral sofa. "There's a wreath."

There was, a big one with red bulbs and berries. There was a candle nestled in a bed of greenery on the table, too.

Kane walked over to the table. Putting his drink down, he lit a lighter and set the candle ablaze. Then he grinned her way.

"What are you doing?" she asked, not wanting to admit she liked it.

"This is different than any other date I've ever been on." He walked toward her, more like a stroll, a sexy one. She resisted the urge to back up as he came to a stop in front of her.

"What's different about it?"

He exaggerated a shrug. "Oh, I don't know. A city-wide blackout. We're in a hotel suite instead of a coffee shop."

"Yes, that does make it a little different."

"You make it different, too." He was no longer being playful. He was serious.

"Think you're gonna get lucky tonight?" She had to keep this light. She wasn't ready to trust him.

"I'm already lucky. Stranded with a beautiful woman, having a romantic dinner for two on Christmas Eve. Who would've thought?"

"Not me." She sipped her drink again.

"You think all I'm after is sex?"

She didn't know what to think. He hadn't seemed interested in only sex with his date yesterday.

"It isn't. I've been looking a long time for a woman I enjoy talking to. We don't seem to be lacking in that area."

It was easy to talk to him, and there was a wonderful heat to their chemistry. He seemed to understand what she was thinking and feeling without saying much.

"You're just having a hard time accepting it. Because you saw me with so many women."

Weird. "Can't argue there."

"I guess I was going after it a little too aggressively."

"What...the perfect wife?"

"Perfect for me."

"And your career. I don't want a man who puts his career before me."

"I wouldn't do that."

"Wouldn't you?"

Wrapping his fingers around her martini glass above her hand, he took it from her. Her heart beat faster as she watched him put it on the table with his and then return to her.

"I thought that's the kind of woman I needed," he said. "It wasn't until I met you that I realized what a mistake that would be."

"Are you saying you'd change your work schedule for the right woman?"

"Yes. I'd put her first."

Oh, this was getting dangerously good. Dare she dream of being the right woman for him?

He stepped closer, sending her pulse flying.

"I'm curious," he said.

"Uh-oh."

He chuckled. "That guy you were with for...what did you say? Ten years?"

"Yeah."

"You ended it, right?"

"Yes." Why was he bringing this up now?

"So it can't be him that made you standoffish."

"I'm not—"

"And the online dates," he interrupted. "Most of them were just one or two dates, right?"

"...e of them lasted longer."

"...d you love any of them?"

"...No! Of course not."

He smiled and she realized what she'd given away. Her defensiveness spoke loudest of all.

"You loved the last one you were with."

No, she hadn't. "I thought I did."

"What are you so afraid of, Shanna Toole?" he asked.

Falling in love with the wrong man. But she couldn't say it to him. Uncomfortable, she stepped back and turned, passing a sleeping Scotch on the couch on her way to the window. The city was dark under a starlit sky.

She heard him move to stand behind her, stirring her senses and building heat low in her abdomen.

"Don't be afraid of me, Shanna." His hands glided up her arm and stopped near her shoulders. "How can I hurt you when I feel the same as you?"

She turned and looked up at him, melting into his eyes.

"I won't hurt you," he said. "I want this. I want what I haven't found online or anywhere else."

Oh, God. Yes.

"Do want that, too?" he asked. "Do you want what you haven't found?"

"Yes." It came out on a sultry breath.

He slid his hand along her side to her back. Pulling her against him, he brought his head just above hers.

"I'm going to kiss you."

Her breathing quickened and she tipped her head back a little. Anticipating. Humming with it. She felt outside herself, full of wanting so powerful she swam in it.

He did kiss her, a featherlight touch at first, then with more pressure. He brushed his lips over hers. His tongue tantalized her. She opened her mouth and he took it with his, sweeping in for a deeper kiss. Her breath tripped into a more needy rhythm, his sounding the same.

The lights went dark.

Kane pulled back and she searched around the suite. The only light came from the single candle burning on the table.

"What happened?" she asked, even though she knew.

"Must be having problems with the generator."

She looked through the windows but couldn't see much. Dark shapes of buildings blocked some of her view of the stars.

When she moved her head to peer up at Kane, her eyes had adjusted enough to see him watching her. His striking green eyes enticed her. The fire of his passion ignited her own. She leaned against him and angled her mouth over his.

She slid her arms over his shoulders. A tingling glow started in the region of her heart and now pooled between her legs. This connection that had sprung between them erupted like sticks of dynamite.

He lifted her and started to walk. She hitched her knees on his hips as he carried her to the couch. Scotch groaned and jumped off, trotting to a chair and hopping up onto that, curling onto a ball.

Shanna lay on her back on the couch and Kane lowered himself on top of her. The weight of him felt delicious. His long, lean body pressed in all the right places against hers. She wrapped her arms around his neck as his mouth toyed with hers. His tongue a fluid dance keeping tune to the sensual rhythm. Never had she been with a man who matched her like this, on such an intimate level. Already.

He rose up and pulled off his shirt. She put her hands on his stomach and ran them over his chest, feeling his pebbled nipples. He came back down and pressed his mouth to hers, resuming his magic. His hardness pressing where she craved him made her open her legs. Groaning, he kissed her neck, tongue wetting a trail of heat down the V of her blouse.

Too fast.

His fingers unbuttoned one, then two buttons.

"Kane."

"I want to be inside you."

"Oh." The thought of that filled her with animalistic need. She lifted her hips against his hardness.

He moved down, taking his erection away from her. She moaned a protest, raking her fingers into his hair. His mouth touched what he'd exposed of her stomach. He unbuttoned the rest of her blouse.

It was like she was watching herself as she sat up and let him remove the garment and unhook her bra. Now she was bare from the waist up. She lay back on the couch, raising her arms above her head, her forearms on the armrest. He looked down at her, knees between her legs, a man hungry for the taste of his woman.

Putting his hands on each side of her, he kissed her. The tenderness of it sent tingles all the way to her toes. His mouth slid off hers and moved to her neck again. He groaned.

Too fast. Too soon.

"Kane."

"I know," he rasped. "Don't worry. Don't be afraid."

His mouth came back to hers. The building urgency swept her to neverland. That spark between them that had ignited out of nowhere as soon as the lights had gone out flared.

She felt his hands on the waist of her jeans and lifted her head to watch him. He kissed her stomach, his tongue doing circles there, sending sensation ricocheting across her skin and deeper. She got dizzy with it.

He unzipped her jeans and started to pull them down. His green eyes lifted to meet hers. "Just the jeans."

She nodded. He left her underwear on as he removed her jeans. He stood from the couch and removed his own jeans, leaving on his green plaid boxers. She could see his erection pushing out the material. Parting her legs as he came back down on her, she groaned when she felt his hardness against her, only their underwear separating their bare flesh.

He kissed her for endless moments, moving his hips, rubbing against her, stroking her closer and closer to orgasm. She parted her legs wider and lifted her knees, earning herself the sound of a hungry groan from him. Holding his head with both hands, loving the feel of his hair between her fingers, she tipped her head back to catch her breath. He kissed her neck, sucking a little before crawling down her body, planting wet kisses as he went, taking his time at her nipples before moving on to her ribs and stomach.

She wanted to watch him but sensation made her dig her head back into the couch and arch her back. Kane curled his fingers against her skin as he took hold of the hem of her underwear. She lifted her head in time to see him look up at her, his eyes on fire with want. It drove her over the edge.

He pulled her underwear down just a little. An inch.

More.

His tongue explored what he'd exposed.

More.

Still watching her, he pulled her underwear down another inch. He was almost there, teasing the perimeter of what yearned for him. She relaxed against the pillow, putting her arms above her head again, looking at him. She felt drugged with anticipation. He pulled her underwear down more, exposing just enough. His tongue touched her.

The trigger-sharp sensation made her close her eyes and a sound exhaled from her.

He slipped her underwear down more. Totally exposed now. And his tongue found her. An instant later, she came. The most incredible orgasm she'd ever had. She didn't even know if she made any sounds. He'd transported her to oblivion. His answering groan suggested she had.

Pulling her underwear all the way off, he stood and removed his. She thought he'd take her right there on the couch. She was feeling enough like a wet noodle to let him. But instead he bent and lifted her, carrying her naked to the bedroom.

Depositing her on the bed, he kneed her legs apart. He didn't wait. Propped above her, he drove himself into her and started pumping his hips. She thought he'd continue on that way, bringing her closer to another peak with each thrust, but he didn't. He slowed, easing the crescendo into a tortuous ache, until she felt his penetration everywhere in her body. Sensation numbed her to anything but the feel of him reaching for that deep, elusive place.

He began to groan with each impassioned breath, telling her he was close. His pleasure stimulated hers. She burst from the inside, gripped by the tumultuous release, feeling his at the same time.

He stayed on top of her, catching his breath along with her. It took a while for the sensations singing inside her to calm. She could stay like this for hours. It felt so right. So terrifyingly right.

Chapter 5

Shanna woke slowly. She stretched long and languidly, blinking away sleep. It took her a moment to remember where she was.

Kane.

Last night.

Oh, dear God...how had it happened so fast?

Rolling her head, she saw him lying next to her, the covers down to his waist, one manly hand resting on his abdomen, the other beside his head on the pillow. He was more handsome in the morning light than he'd been to her last night.

She felt her face heat as she recalled how many times they'd made love. Or had that only been sex? They hadn't known each other much longer than a day. And yet it felt as if she had known him all her life.

More than sex.

Would he feel the same?

Uneasiness spread through her. She slinked out of bed, finding her clothes and taking them out into the living room to dress. Hearing the refrigerator in the bar area, she realized that at some point during the night, the power had come back on. Moving to the window, the city sparkled under a clear blue sky.

She couldn't tell if the hotel was running on a generator or if the city had gotten the power restored.

She found the remote and turned on the television. A news program showed a Christmas tree in downtown Seattle, the lights on and twinkling.

"I woke up and you were gone."

She spun around to see Kane standing in only his jeans.

"The power is back on," she said.

He glanced at the television, but his attention returned to her. She began to feel awkward, not knowing how he felt now that it was morning. Hell, she didn't even know how she felt.

"Are you all right?" he asked.

She nodded, feeling ridiculously sensitive.

He walked over to her. Kissed her. And then his green eyes smiled down at her. "Thinking I'm going to run?"

She breathed a laugh. How did he know?

"I'm not." His arms slid around her and he brought her close.

Pressing her cheek against his, she savored the feeling, breathing in his smell. "What happened last night?"

"I don't know. Something good."

She smiled and kissed his cheek.

"I didn't plan it."

"I didn't, either." She kissed him again, marveling how secure she felt doing so.

"I want to keep seeing you."

This was such unfamiliar territory for her. She couldn't remember ever feeling like this with any other man. So good…and…so sure.

But she didn't want to spend the rest of her life with a man who put his work first. Yes, he'd claimed he no longer wanted that, but how long would that last? Would he grow unhappy with a woman who needed him that much?

Meeting Kane, making love with him, made her realize just how close she'd gotten to giving up finding that special someone. She'd stopped believing in herself, that she was worthy of the kind of man she yearned for but had never admitted to wanting. Kane was that kind of man. Worthy of her. And she was worthy of him…but would he recognize that after fishing the sea of women he had?

Disheartened and losing that floating, secure feeling, she pushed away from him and turned toward the window.

"Shanna."

He stood behind her. Reluctantly, she turned.

"I feel the same as you."

She breathed a laugh. "How do you know what I'm feeling?"

"I was in bed with you last night."

"What am I feeling, then?" He had a magical way of pulling her out of her sadness and turning it into happiness.

"You're wondering if this is going to last. You've gone on so many dates that part of you expects it to end."

She nodded. He was amazing.

"Well, I want it to last."

Her throat tightened with emotion. "So do I."

A lopsided grin shaped his mouth. "Wait here."

Perplexed, she watched him go to the bar and open a cabinet. When he straightened, he held a wrapped gift the size of a shirt box.

She looked from it to his face. He'd gotten her a Christmas present? She was too stunned to move.

He approached with a grin as though he knew. He knew too much about her already.

She took the present.

"Open it," he coaxed, sounding pleased with himself.

"I didn't get you anything." She hadn't even thought to. Did that make her selfish?

"You can get me one next year."

The reference to such a far-off day told her just how invested he was in this. Looking up at him, she laughed. Taking the gift to the couch, she sat and opened the ends first, and then tore enough of the wrapping to expose the box.

"How did you get this wrapped?" she asked as she pulled the white shirt box free.

"Had some at my office."

She sent him a quick glance. "You have wrapping paper at your office?"

"My assistant does."

Smiling, she dropped the wrapping paper and opened the box. Inside lay papers. A contract. A rental contract.

Shanna went still, so stunned she could barely process what this meant. She'd thought he'd gone to the office to work on Christmas Eve, but he'd gone to draft her a new contract. The onslaught of tears burned her nose and moisture sprang to her eyes.

She looked up at him, speechless against the power of her emotion. No one had ever done anything like this for her before. Gone so far out of their way just for her. All the years she'd struggled with dating, feeling so alone and unwanted, and now this. It was worth the wait.

"I read the one you signed and I agree—it's not a fair contract," he said. "I pay my managers commission on the contracts they sign, but only to encourage them to get a lot of them signed. They have strict instructions not to gouge anyone, but in your case the manager gouged. You weren't the only one. I'm going to fire him after the holiday."

Shanna lowered her eyes and read the terms. She couldn't believe it. He'd lowered her rent below what it had been before she signed the renewal.

"All you have to do is sign," he said.

She looked up at him again. His eyes glowed in the morning light, meeting her gaze with satisfaction and what might turn out to be love. She took in the rest of him, the hair on his chest that tapered to a line down his stomach, the shape of his groin in the jeans, his bare feet. She couldn't believe he wanted her. But the way he'd made love to her last night, and his thoughtfulness in giving her this present, was enough to convince her he did.

She was no longer afraid of falling in love with him.

Putting the box on the couch beside her, she stood and walked to him, launching herself against him. When he caught her, she wrapped her legs around him and started kissing his face, the corners of his eyes, his nose, his cheeks, his mouth. His arms felt delicious around her waist, holding her effortlessly, making her feel light and airy.

"Thank you," she breathed.

He walked toward the bedroom. "Don't thank me yet."

"Mmm…is it time for your present now?"

"Yes. How many are you prepared to give me?"

"As many as you want. However and wherever you want them, too."

"Oh my God…"

She laughed. "Merry Christmas."

He lowered her onto the unmade bed. "Merry Christmas."

There was that energy again, growing stronger, sweeping her into the light of new love. "Kiss me."

And he did.

* * * * *

*Celebrate 60 years of pure reading pleasure
with Harlequin®!
Just in time for the holidays,
Silhouette Special Edition®
is proud to present* New York Times *bestselling author
Kathleen Eagle's
ONE COWBOY, ONE CHRISTMAS.*

Rodeo rider Zach Beaudry was a travelin' man—until he
broke down in middle-of-nowhere South Dakota during
a deep freeze. That's when an angel came to his rescue....

'Don't die on me. Come on, Zel. You know how much I love you, girl. You're all I've got. Don't do this to me here. Not *now*."

But Zelda had quit on him, and Zach Beaudry had no one to blame but himself. He'd taken his sweet time hitting the road, and then miscalculated a shortcut. For all he knew he was a hundred miles from gas. But even if they were sitting next to a pump, the ten dollars he had in his pocket wouldn't get him out of South Dakota, which was not where he wanted to be right now. Not even his beloved pickup truck, Zelda, could get him much of anywhere on fumes. He was sitting out in the cold in the middle of nowhere. And getting colder.

He shifted the pickup into Neutral and pulled hard on the steering wheel, using the downhill slope to get her off the blacktop and into the roadside grass, where she shuddered to a standstill. He stroked the padded dash. "You'll be safe here."

But Zach would not. It was getting dark, and it was already too damn cold for his cowboy ass. Zach's battered body was a barometer, and he was feeling South Dakota, big-time. He'd have given his right arm to be climbing into a hotel hot tub instead of a brutal blast of north wind. The right was his free arm anyway. Damn thing had lost altitude, touched some part of the bull and caused him a scoreless ride last time out.

It wasn't scoring him a ride this night, either. A carload of teenagers whizzed by, topping off the insult by laying on the horn as they passed him. It was at least twenty minutes before another vehicle came along. He stepped out and waved both arms this time, damn near getting himself killed. Whatever happened to *do unto others?* In places like this, decent people didn't leave each other stranded in the cold.

His face was feeling stiff, and he figured he'd better start walking before his toes went numb. He struck out for a distant yard light, the only sign of human habitation in sight. He couldn't tell how distant, but he knew he'd be hurting by the time he got there, and he was counting on some kindly old man to be answering the door. No shame among the lame.

It wasn't like Zach was fresh off the operating table—it had been a few months since his last round of repairs—but he hadn't given himself enough time. He'd lopped a couple of weeks off the near end of the doc's estimated recovery time, rigged up a brace, done some heavy-duty taping and climbed onto another bull. Hung in there for five seconds—four seconds past feeling the pop in his hip and three seconds short of the buzzer.

He could still feel the pain shooting down his leg with every step. Only this time he had to pick the damn thing up, swing it forward and drop it down again on his own.

Pride be damned, he just hoped *somebody* would be answering the door at the end of the road. The light in the front window was a good sign.

The four steps to the covered porch might as well have been four hundred, and he was looking to climb them with a lead weight chained to his left leg. His eyes were just as screwed up as his hip. Big black spots danced around with tiny red flashers, and he couldn't tell what was real and what wasn't. He stumbled over some shrubbery, steadied himself on the porch railing and peered between vertical slats.

There in the front window stood a spruce tree with a silver star affixed to the top. Zach was pretty sure the red sparks were all in his head, but the white lights twinkling by the hundreds throughout the huge tree, those were real. He wasn't too sure about the woman hanging the shiny balls. Most of her hair was caught up on her head and fastened in a curly clump, but the light captured by the escaped bits crowned her with a golden halo. Her face was a soft shadow, her body a willowy silhouette beneath a long white gown. If this was where the mind ran off to when cold started shutting down the rest of the body, then Zach's final worldly thought was, *This ain't such a bad way to go.*

If she would just turn to the window, he could die looking into the eyes of a Christmas angel.

* * * * *

*Could this woman from Zach's past get the lonesome
cowboy to come in from the cold...for good?
Look for*
ONE COWBOY, ONE CHRISTMAS
*by Kathleen Eagle.
Available December 2009 from
Silhouette Special Edition®.*

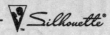

SPECIAL EDITION

FROM *NEW YORK TIMES* AND *USA TODAY*
BESTSELLING AUTHOR

KATHLEEN EAGLE

ONE COWBOY,
One Christmas

When bull rider Zach Beaudry appeared
out of thin air on Ann Drexler's ranch,
she thought she was seeing a ghost of
Christmas past. And though Zach had
no memory of their night of passion years
ago, they were about to share a future
he would never forget.

Available December 2009
wherever books are sold.

SSE65493

REQUEST YOUR FREE BOOKS!

2 FREE NOVELS PLUS 2 FREE GIFTS!

Silhouette® Romantic

SUSPENSE

Sparked by Danger, Fueled by Passion!

YES! Please send me 2 FREE Silhouette® Romantic Suspense novels and my 2 FREE gifts (gifts are worth about $10). After receiving them, if I don't wish to receive any more books, I can return the shipping statement marked "cancel." If I don't cancel, I will receive 4 brand-new novels every month and be billed just $4.24 per book in the U.S. or $4.99 per book in Canada. That's a savings of at least 15% off the cover price! It's quite a bargain! Shipping and handling is just 50¢ per book*. I understand that accepting the 2 free books and gifts places me under no obligation to buy anything. I can always return a shipment and cancel at any time. Even if I never buy another book from Silhouette, the two free books and gifts are mine to keep forever.

240 SDN EYL4   340 SDN EYMG

Name _____ (PLEASE PRINT) _____

Address _____ Apt. # _____

City _____ State/Prov. _____ Zip/Postal Code _____

Signature (if under 18, a parent or guardian must sign)

Mail to the **Silhouette Reader Service:**
IN U.S.A.: P.O. Box 1867, Buffalo, NY 14240-1867
IN CANADA: P.O. Box 609, Fort Erie, Ontario L2A 5X3

Not valid to current subscribers of Silhouette Romantic Suspense books.

Want to try two free books from another line?
Call 1-800-873-8635 or visit www.morefreebooks.com.

* Terms and prices subject to change without notice. Prices do not include applicable taxes. Sales tax applicable in N.Y. Canadian residents will be charged applicable provincial taxes and GST. Offer not valid in Quebec. This offer is limited to one order per household. All orders subject to approval. Credit or debit balances in a customer's account(s) may be offset by any other outstanding balance owed by or to the customer. Please allow 4 to 6 weeks for delivery. Offer available while quantities last.

Your Privacy: Silhouette is committed to protecting your privacy. Our Privacy Policy is available online at www.eHarlequin.com or upon request from the Reader Service. From time to time we make our lists of customers available to reputable third parties who may have a product or service of interest to you. If you would prefer we not share your name and address, please check here. ☐

SRS09R

Silhouette®
Romantic
SUSPENSE

COMING NEXT MONTH
Available November 24, 2009

#1587 THE CAVANAUGH CODE—Marie Ferrarella
Cavanaugh Justice
When detective Taylor McIntyre discovers a suspicious man lurking around a crime scene, she never guesses he'll be her new partner on the case. But the moment J. C. Laredo sweeps into the squad room, Taylor can't deny the attraction she feels for the P.I. As they work the nights away, growing ever closer to catching the killer, will they finally give in to the love that's been building inside?

#1588 THE SOLDIER'S SECRET DAUGHTER—Cindy Dees
Top Secret Deliveries
Her mystery man disappeared after their one night of passion, but he left Emily Grainger with a constant reminder—their daughter. So when she receives a tip that leads her to a ship's container, she's shocked to discover her long-lost love held captive inside! Now on the run from his captors, Jagger Holtz will do anything to protect his newly discovered family.

#1589 SEDUCED BY THE OPERATIVE—Merline Lovelace
Code Name: Danger
The president's daughter is having strange dreams, and psychologist Claire Cantwell has been tasked with finding their cause. In a desperate race against time, she and Colonel Luis Esteban follow a mysterious trail halfway around the world. As they face a lethal killer, can they also learn to face their own demons and give in to the love they clearly feel for each other?

#1590 PROTECTING THEIR BABY—Sheri WhiteFeather
Warrior Society
After her first and only one-night stand, Lisa Gordon suddenly finds herself pregnant...and in danger. Rex Sixkiller enjoys his free-spirited life, but when Lisa and his unborn child are threatened, he takes action. As the threats escalate and Rex fights to keep them safe, he and Lisa also wage a losing battle to protect their hearts.

SRSCNMBPA1109